HOW TO BE ANGRY AT CHRISTMAS

BETH RAIN

CHAPTER ONE

'TIS THE SEASON TO BE JOLLY, BUT IF YOU'RE NOT FEELING IT – LET THE "BAH HUMBUGS" OUT TO PLAY!

'*I* know you're up here somewhere!'

I eyeball the deep darkness in front of me, doing my best not to wobble. My legs are starting to shake and my kneecaps are protesting from being rammed against a rung as I attempt to stay anchored to the ladder.

I'm halfway through the hatch that leads to the attic, peering into the chilly gloom ahead of me. What on earth was I thinking, coming up here in the middle of the night?! A shiver tiptoes down my spine. Maybe this isn't such a great idea after all? Shapes loom in front of me and my breath catches in my throat. I *really* don't like this.

I've got two choices - I could chicken out and head straight back downstairs. It's warm down there and there's a mostly-decorated Christmas tree waiting to greet me. Or… I could woman-up and get on with my mission.

Option two. It has to be option two!

I haul myself through the hatch onto the dusty boards and take a long, slow, calming breath. I'll find that package if it's the last thing I do!

'Worst choice of words ever!' I gulp, fumbling around for the heavy torch I tossed up here before white-knuckling my way up the ladder.

As my fingers find its reassuring bulk, I hurry to flick the switch - desperate for the comfort of some light. The narrow beam does little to calm my fears… if anything, it makes the attic look even more like the set of a horror movie.

I swallow as a headless dressmaker's dummy catches my eye.

'Come on Holly,' I mutter. 'It's just an attic!'

Just a dusty, dark, slightly creaky attic. There isn't anything to be scared of up here. That dummy – or *Freaky Frieda* as my best friend Linda named her - is nothing more than a reminder of a hobby that lasted all of three seconds. Oh - and the fact that I really shouldn't be allowed access to my credit cards after watching TV programs full of super-crafty people who just happen to be ridiculously talented too.

I am *not* crafty… and the less said about my talents - or lack thereof - the better!

'Focus Holly!'

All I need to do is find the package I came up here

for and then I can hot-foot it back downstairs. I might even treat myself to a sherry as a reward for my bravery. Or… *another sherry* I should say!

Scrambling to my feet, I keep my head slightly bent so that I don't end up headbutting one of the low rafters. I swing the heavy torch in a giant arc, doing my best to illuminate as much of the attic as I can in one go. Dusty boxforts jump out at me from every direction as I do my best to get my bearings.

'Don't freak out, don't freak out!' I chant in a kind of mantra as my eyes rake the jumble in front of me.

Okay, I know I'm being ridiculous right now. This is my cottage and I'm a grown woman. But… to be fair… I've recently come to the conclusion that this doesn't mean the same thing as "grown-up" - as evidenced by my incredibly dodgy decision to climb a rickety ladder and embark on a solo adventure to the attic when there's no one else around.

Still… that's the joy of being single, isn't it? There's never anyone around these days… other than old Eileen in the cottage next door, and I doubt she'd be able to hear me if I did need to shout for help!

I have to admit – coming up here on my own is a bit of a… bold move. Especially as it's gone midnight and I've been quite enthusiastic about toasting Grandpa Alf's memory with his favourite sherry while trimming my Christmas tree.

That's what kicked off this little adventure in the first place. Waiting for me downstairs is the first

Christmas tree I've had in years. A proper, real tree. The kind my idiot ex wouldn't let anywhere near the house. It's big and bushy and smells divine – and it deserves the best of the best when it comes to baubles. Unfortunately for me – those are hiding up here somewhere in one of these boxes. It's where I stashed all Gramps's things when I lost him... so they've got to be here somewhere!

I take another deep, calming breath and then promptly start to cough as I inhale about a decade's worth of dust.

'Nice!' I splutter. 'Very calming!'

The sooner I get this done, the better. I turn to the stack of boxes closest to me and do my best to hold the torch steady so that I can see what's scrawled on them in thick, black marker.

'Colin kitchen. Colin toys. Colin personal!' I mutter as my eyes become accustomed to the half-light. You know, I could swear I told that cheating, conniving-

I take another deep breath and cough again. There's no point getting worked up. I refuse to get angry – it's just not my style. But I distinctly remember threatening my ex-husband with a skip if he didn't remove all his shi- rubbish before the end of September.

It's now December.

Late enough in December that we're coming up to the last Christmas posting date. It's definitely time for that skip... or maybe I could have a bonfire instead - that would be a lot more fun!

Either way, it's not going to help me right now, is it?! The fact that there's still a ton of Colin's junk up here is just going to make my mission even harder. I aim a little kick at one of his boxes as I creep past them towards a pile of old suitcases.

'Git!' I mutter.

Considering this is my first Christmas on my own, I've been doing pretty well at keeping all thoughts of my idiot ex-husband firmly at bay so far. Or *almost*-ex, I should say. The divorce is well and truly underway - but I can't wait to get that final paperwork signed, sealed and settled. I know there's not much chance of it happening in time for Christmas now, but still… a girl can dream. It would certainly be a much better present than the one I got last year!

'Deck the halls with boughs of HOLLY!'

Even though the horrifically off-key warble comes out of my own mouth, it's so loud in the confined space that I jump and send a stack of old diaries tumbling off their perch.

'Idiot!' I laugh.

The loud noise does the trick, though – for a moment or two, at least. I've managed to banish the collywobbles and - more importantly - I'm not thinking about *him* anymore. I'm right in the middle of spending a pretty magical evening in my own company - and there's no way I'm going to let that good-for-nothing grinch ruin my twinkle-fest. Not this year!

'Fa la la la LAAA!' I add for good measure,

scootching down so that I can rummage through some smaller packages that have been shunted right to the edge of the space under the eaves. None of them look quite right, though. I've got a feeling I'll know the box I'm looking for the minute I spot it. After all – Gramps wrapped it, so it's bound to be covered in his signature brown paper and knotted-string combo!

Even so, I flip open one of the flaps on the box nearest to me and do my best to angle the torchlight so that I can peep inside. Nope. It looks like it's just a nest of spare tea towels.

Scuttling backwards like a crab, I straighten up as far as I can without getting covered in cobwebs. Then I let out a huge yawn for good measure. I'm tired, and the idea of disappearing back downstairs is getting more tempting by the second.

I'd forgotten how much of Gramps's stuff I stashed up here without sorting through it. At the time, I just didn't have it in me – not with my marriage busily imploding just to add to my misery.

'I'm not giving up!' I huff, even as I realise it could take forever to find what I'm looking for up here. But… I'm not a quitter! I've promised myself a wonderful Christmas – and Christmas won't be Christmas without this final festive touch.

I turn towards the monstrous mannequin at the far end of the attic and roll my eyes. It's bound to be over there somewhere, isn't it? As much as I hate the idea, it looks like I'm going to have to get up close and personal with *Freaky Frieda*.

'Come on Gramps, help me find it so I can go back downstairs!' I whisper, creeping across the creaking boards as though I might disturb the snoozing mannequin if I'm too loud.

I climb carefully over a pink plastic washing basket filled to the brim with ancient VHS tapes. Why I saved this lot is anyone's guess… maybe it's not just Colin who needs a bit of skip-action in the new year!

Grabbing the frayed handle of a giant, squashy laundry bag, I'm just about to start shifting it out of the way when my foot catches in the corner of an old, motheaten throw, and I give it an almighty yank. There's an ominous grinding sound.

'Noooo!' I gasp, dropping the torch as I turn to lunge for the ornate mirror that must have been hiding underneath the dusty cloth. I just manage to catch it before it crashes face-down onto the boards.

Phew – disaster averted!

Getting a better grip on its heavy wooden frame, I shift the mirror and lean it safely against yet another stack of cardboard boxes. I'm just about to cover it with the throw again when I catch sight of something reflected in its depths. Right at *Freaky Frieda's* feet – illuminated perfectly by the beam of light from my dropped torch – is a box. It's covered with faded brown paper, held in place by several loops of knotted string.

'Bingo!' I say with a grin. 'Cheers Gramps!'

CHAPTER TWO

ANGER IS LIKE SHERRY - TOO MUCH, AND YOU'LL REGRET IT!

The minute my feet leave the ladder and hit cosy hallway carpet, I breathe a sigh of relief. I've made it out of the attic in one piece, and what's more – so has my precious package! For a second, I stand and stare at the ladder. It wouldn't hurt just to leave it where it is and put it away in the morning, would it?

'Maybe not!' I mutter as an image of *Freaky Frieda* making a break for freedom pops into my head. Without wasting another second, I release the catches and fold the ladder up out of the way. Then - with much grunting and a couple of less-than-festive swear words thrown in for good measure – I manage to wiggle the hatch cover back into position, blocking her escape route.

'Ha! So long Frieda!' I say, shooting a triumphant

little salute at the ceiling before grabbing my box again and heading for the stairs.

As soon as I catch sight of my newly-Christmassy-fied bannisters, the last of the shivery, dusty darkness falls away. I grin at my gorgeous decorations. Sure, they might be a little bit wonky here and there, but I'm super-chuffed with them. They are… a *lot!* I'm pulling out all the stops this year. Now there's no one here to stop me – I can finally let my little festive freak flag fly!

Floating down the stairs, I brush my hand lightly over the tartan garlands dotted with golden pinecones and fresh, deep-green boughs. I can't believe it's been so long since I've properly celebrated Christmas.

What was I thinking?

I know hindsight is a wonderful thing, but I'm not sure I'd have agreed to marry Colin in the first place if I'd realised how much the idiot hates Christmas! He is anti-decorations, anti-presents, and definitely anti-fun! The man has this incredible ability to suck all the joy out of my favourite time of year…okay, okay - out of *any* time of year, if I'm being completely honest!

Of course – his shenanigans last Christmas were his pièce de résistance – a true masterpiece in misery.

'Anyway, moving on!' I say in a loud, cheerful voice. Sure… it's a little bit forced, but I'm done wasting any more time thinking about him. Plus, I've got a tree to finish off… and what a tree it is!

Getting the ginormous Norwegian Spruce home

from the Christmas market was interesting, to say the least. The guys I bought it from were very helpful and tied it to the top of the car for me. Unfortunately, I didn't quite factor in the fact that I'd have to drag it back down on my own. It was… an experience - one I'll be reminded of every time I see those lovely long scratches in my poor old car's glossy red paintwork.

Was it worth it?

Is Santa fat and jolly?!

If I'm being honest, the tree wasn't the only thing I splashed out on while I was there. In fact, I'm not sure the Christmas market knew what hit it. I came home with half a forest's worth of greenery and pine cones in the boot, and there's going to be a tartan ribbon shortage for the foreseeable future!

Bouncing through to the living room, I pause to admire the sight as a wave of pure, Christmas-fuelled nostalgia washes over me. I swear there's no other feeling on Earth that comes close to rummaging through boxes of baubles and tinsel, hunting for your favourites.

The room twinkles merrily back at me - a delicious muddle of reds, greens and every other colour I could lay my hands on. I know loads of people love to colour co-ordinate their Christmases, but that's never been my style. The more it looks like the inside of a box of chocolates - with their gleaming, jewel-bright wrappers, the happier I am.

I take a deep sniff of the warm, pine-scented air, then let out a huge sigh of contentment. I know, I know… I really shouldn't be feeling *quite* this happy considering it's my first Christmas officially alone – but frankly, I'm just thrilled to be done with all those barren, bauble-free years at last! I'd almost forgotten how it feels to put up a Christmas tree and then weave its branches with tinsel and memories of years gone by.

Sniffing the air again, I catch the sweet scent of sherry mingling with the pine. Maybe it's time for another little glass… after all – it's what Gramps would have wanted!

I make my way over to the coffee table and pop my parcel down next to a jumble of ribbons. Then, grabbing the half-empty blue glass bottle from the sideboard, I ease out the stopper and trickle some of the amber liquid into the waiting glass.

'I miss you, Gramps,' I say, lifting it and toasting the tree before taking a delicate sip.

I'd better do my best to make this one last… I could do without a hangover for my pre-work coffee date with Linda in the morning. My best friend has seen me in various states of disrepair this year - what with grief and impending divorce taking it in turns to give me a good thumping - but there's no need to subject her to hungover-Holly just before Christmas

On that note, it's time to finish off the tree… and then head for bed!

Kneeling down next to the coffee table, I grab the package again. It's time to untie the string... but as much as I want to get at what's waiting for me inside – I hesitate and run my fingertips over the knots. Gramps wrapped this, and part of me wants to keep it exactly as it is.

Don't be daft, my girl – nothing stays the same forever – get on with it!

His voice sounds so clear inside my head that I jump and then let out a surprised laugh. The man was nothing if not practical! Taking the slightly spooky advice, I get to work on the various knots and then unwrap the folds of brown paper to reveal the familiar, faded-blue box. The cardboard is fragile and silky-soft with age. Easing the lid off gently, I stare down at the treasures inside.

So... that's where Christmas has been hiding all these years!

Perfect golds, reds, silvers and blues twinkle up at me as I gaze at the vintage glass baubles, nestled in their beds of ancient cotton wool. For me - these little gems represent the beginning of Christmas. Nan and Gramps would save this box until I arrived at their house on Christmas Eve. Then Gramps would help me hang them on the tree while Nan dashed off to the kitchen to rustle up a plate full of treats - along with a glass of milk for me and a sherry for Gramps.

'I miss you guys!' I whisper, blinking hard as my

eyes fill with hot tears and the twinkling lights around me bloom into stars.

Biting my lip in an attempt to stop it from wobbling, I reach into the box for my favourite ornament and hold it up to the light. Palest blue, silver and frosted white, it spins gently in the warmth of the pine-scented air for a moment before I hang it carefully right at the front of my gorgeous, bushy tree.

'There you go, Gramps,' I say, my voice thick with unshed tears, 'this one's for you.'

I'm just about to choose another bauble when the pile of leftover ribbon on the coffee table starts to vibrate, breaking the spell and scaring the living daylights out of me.

So *that's* where my mobile phone got to! Who on earth is calling at this time of night?! Rummaging through the cheerful mess, I grab it and stare at the name on the screen.

Ex-Dumbass – Do Not Answer

Linda insisted if I was going to keep his number, I had to at least save it under a more appropriate name.

Nooo! What's Colin doing, calling me in the middle of the night?!

I should just ignore it, shouldn't I? I mean… the man's ruined enough of my life already, there's no way I'm going to let him spoil tonight too.

But… if I let it go to voicemail… I know I'll just worry.

It's really late…

What if it's something serious?!

'Hello?' I say, accepting the call before I can think better of it.

'Where have you been?' demands Colin, sounding decidedly stroppy. 'I've been calling and texting for ages! Why didn't you answer?!'

'Sorry… I was…' I pause. No - Colin doesn't get to know what I've been doing. It isn't anything to do with him anymore. 'What do you want?'

'Don't be like that, Holly Berry!' he hiccups.

I promptly make violent puking gestures to the room at large… not that there's anyone here to appreciate my comedy genius. The old pet name that used to make me smile now just makes me all squirmy instead.

Colin hiccups again. He's clearly wasted.

I sigh. 'What do you want?'

'Look… I…' he pauses and takes a dramatic, shaky breath. All it does is make me roll my eyes. I *really* should have just let it go to voicemail.

'Me and Marcia… we broke up.'

'So?' I say.

I don't want to sound completely heartless… but what else does he expect from me? After all - Marcia's *the other woman*. She's the reason I spent last Christmas doing a very good impression of Frosty the Snowman on a sunbed! *The tears… oh the tears!*

'Look,' says Colin again, clearly trying to sound both sane and sober. It's a weird habit of his - and usually a sure sign he's already passed *mildly-pissed* and heading rapidly towards *falling-down-drunk*. 'I think we need to talk.'

'Well… go and talk to her then,' I huff. 'I'm not stopping you!'

I really don't need this right now - he's totally killing my festive buzz!

'Not *me-and-her* we,' says Colin. '*You-and-me* we! It was all a mistake. A big mistake.'

He pauses and then lets out a long, loud burp followed by another hiccup. 'We should give it another try, Jolly-Holly-Dolly.'

'I don't think so!' I say, wrinkling my nose. I'm quite proud of how definite I sound - and instantly wish Linda was here to witness it. She's always on at me for being too soft.

'We've still got a chance to make things work,' he wheedles in what he clearly thinks is a winning tone.

It's really not – it just makes me want to do mean things to his fingernails with a pair of pliers.

'I'll come over,' he says. 'You've got something to drink in the house, right?!'

'Not tonight, Colin,' I say quickly, shuddering at the idea of him rocking up at the front door, uninvited, and crashing into my lovely, Christmassy wonderland.

'Why are you always so bloody unreasonable?' he huffs. 'I've got nowhere else to go, and things are so hard at this time of year. I could come over and we could talk and then-'

I hit the big red button and cut my almost-ex-husband off mid-sentence. Whatever he was about to say, I'm not falling for it. At least… not this time around!

CHAPTER THREE

KEEP YOUR FRIENDS CLOSE AND YOUR
ANGER CLOSER. IT'S JUST LOOKING FOR A
WARM HUG AND A HOT CHOCOLATE BY
THE FIRE

a blast of pastry-scented air swirls out to greet
me as I yank open the door of the coffee
shop. It's practically enough to make me go weak at the
knees. After last night's sherry-fest – I'm desperate for
a bit of sugar and caffeine to jump-start my day.

I adore this place. It's like something lifted straight
out of the 1950s – right down to the staff uniforms – a
fabulous mix of wiggle dresses, circle skirts and denim.
The art on the walls is neon, and the vibe is always
upbeat.

Linda and I have become such regular visitors over
the past six months that we're on first-name terms
with all the waitresses. Our favourite table is always
reserved for our pre-work powwow – and we're both
invited to the owner's wedding next summer. Suze has
just about got used to me and Linda punctuating our
early-morning gossip sessions by warbling along to the

café's radio… something that's definitely getting more enthusiastic the closer we get to Christmas. She *might* have made us promise that we'd hold off on our impromptu karaoke at her wedding though… on pain of being cut off from our caffeine supply!

Stepping inside, I quickly close the door behind me and wrap my arms around myself in a bid to warm up. I swear the chilly breeze has tiny frost particles in it this morning – my eyebrows feel a bit like they've been flash-frozen. As the café's fragrant warmth curls around me, I do my best to dodge a massive yawn as it tries to body-snatch me.

Last night got late… very late! It was *so* worth it though. I don't think I've stopped smiling since I came downstairs this morning only to come face-to-face with my perfectly decorated tree. Leaving my brand-new – slightly wonky – holly wreath swinging behind me on the front door has definitely added a festive spring to my step… even if it was nearly dawn by the time I put the finishing touches to it.

Rubbing my eyes, I do my best to peer around the long queue of eager caffeine hunters. Blimey – it's heaving in here this morning and every single table seems to be full-to-bursting! I scan the crowd, doing my best to see if Linda's managed to commandeer our favourite table. Somehow, I can't imagine anyone's going to pay much notice to a little "reserved" sign when it's this busy in here!

Ah ha!

I might not be able to see her face… but I'm pretty sure that's Linda's hand waving at me from behind a table full of school kids.

'Blimey!' I gasp, edging my way between the tables until I reach my best friend – who's somehow managed to ensconce herself in our favourite spot despite the hoards.

'Morning!' she grins at me. 'Shove my bags on the floor - they're only there to stop anyone nicking your chair!'

'What are the chances Suze will be able to get to us before we have to leave for work?' I say, doing my best to shrug out of my coat without taking anyone's eye out with my elbows.

'Pretty good - considering I ordered for us about twenty minutes ago!' says Linda. 'I hope you don't mind – I just asked for your usual. Poor Suze is run off her feet - but she promised she'd get to us before we have to leave!'

'You're a hero,' I say, handing Linda her bags and then plopping down into my chair. 'You know that, right?'

'I do!' Linda gives me a wicked wink.

'Hey,' I eyeball her candy-striped jumper dress and immaculate makeup, 'isn't it your office party today?'

Linda works as the office manager for a large firm that does stuff with finance. That's all I know because she never wants to talk about it – claiming it's boring enough to make watching paint dry thrilling in comparison. It started as a temp job about five years ago... and she's still there. Their office parties are legendary, though – mainly because she organises them.

'Yep!' she says with a grin. 'It's party day. Highlight of my year. And... that's why I've got this with me...'

I watch as she rummages around in her handbag, only to pull out a headband - complete with an over-sized sprig of mistletoe suspended on a spring.

'Tasteful!' I chuckle. 'Put it on – let's see!'

'Erm... nope!' Linda wrinkles her nose at me. 'It's a bit early in the day for all that yet. I don't need any unexpected snoggage before I've had my morning coffee. Anyway - I'm holding out for Danny in accounts!'

'Of course you are!' I snort. Danny in accounts has been on the radar ever since he joined the company earlier this year... and as far as I can tell, he's the only thing keeping my friend even vaguely interested in turning up for work.

'Ever hopeful!' Linda winks at me. 'Anyway – how are things at the factory? Are Alf's Angels still in a strop with you?'

I roll my eyes and nod.

Unlike Linda, I adore my job – I mean, who wouldn't want to spend their days at the cutest chocolate factory ever invented? Of course, there's the added bonus that Billingham's Finest Chocolates is now *my* factory... what with me being Holly

Billingham. However – it's not something I've quite wrapped my head around yet. Alf Billingham – or Gramps as he's always been to me – left some seriously large shoes to fill. He also left behind a dedicated workforce – known lovingly as Alf's Angels - and most of them have worked for him from the start.

The Angels keep Billingham's running like a well-oiled machine… even if it's a machine that happens to run on steam power. When I first lost Gramps, they were the glue that helped keep the place together. Hell – they kept me together too! But then something changed… things turned frosty… and I have no idea why.

'Yep,' I sigh. 'I'm still well and truly in the dog house. I just wish I knew why!'

'Hate to mention this, Hols – but you *are* the boss these days,' she says lightly. 'It might be time to… throw your weight around a bit?'

'Are you kidding me?' I laugh. 'For one thing – there's no way I'm ruffling Angel feathers right in the middle of the Christmas rush!'

'Fair point,' says Linda with a shrug.

'And for another thing – Doris and co are flipping terrifying!'

'Wuss!' giggles Linda.

'Too right!' I mutter.

'Coffee ladies!'

A seriously harassed-looking Suze appears at our

table and places a bucket of frothy coffee in front of each of us, along with a gingerbread Santa biscuit.

'You're a sweetheart,' says Linda. 'Thanks Suze!'

'Can't let my regulars down now, can I?' she says with a grin. 'Even when the entire town has decided to descend on me for a pre-work coffee!'

'Yeah - what's going on?' I say, staring around the packed cafe. I don't think I've ever seen it this busy before.

'Erm… it's the week before Christmas?' says Suze with a shrug. 'Happens every year.'

'Yeah,' says Linda through a mouthful of Santa biscuit. 'But Holly here has always missed it because she's been far too busy being married to a Grinch to be allowed to enjoy anything to do with Christmas!'

'Urgh, don't remind me,' I grumble as Suze bustles away to serve the ever-increasing queue.

'Well… it's true,' says Linda. 'Until last year, of course.'

'Hush! I'm doing my best to pretend last year didn't happen,' I say quickly. 'On that note… he called me last night.'

'Eww!' says Linda, pulling a face as if she's just stepped in doggy do-dos.

'Yeah,' I sigh.

'Why?' demands Linda.

'Actually - *when* is more important,' I mutter, 'considering it was after midnight.'

'Please don't tell me you answered that call?' she says, looking even more disgusted.

'It's the week before Christmas,' I say, doing my best not to feel like a kid being told off by a teacher.

'What's that got to do with the price of reindeer poop?' demands Linda.

'I was worried,' I say. 'Something could have been wrong!'

'Holly - I say this with absolute love for you, right?' she says, doing her best to catch my eye and hold my gaze. 'Even if there *was* something wrong - it's soooo not your problem. Not anymore.'

'I know,' I say, shifting uncomfortably in my chair. 'I really *do* know...but-'

'What did he want this time?' she demands, cutting across me. 'My bet is - he's back grovelling again, expecting you to just roll over and let him in?'

I pull a face. I love having a best friend who basically knows me better than I know myself... but sometimes it can be more than a bit inconvenient. The woman's got the memory of an elephant.

'He said he'd split up with his girlfriend,' I say slowly.

'So?!'

'Actually – that was my reaction too!' I say, puffing up proudly. 'He definitely sounded a bit drunk.'

'No surprises there,' grumbles Linda. 'And – just for the record - I don't believe a word of it. Colin's definition of the truth was always very fluid.'

'Don't believe *what?*' I say in surprise. 'You think he was lying about Marcia and him splitting up?' The thought hadn't even occurred to me.

'Wake up and smell the sherry, lovely,' says Linda, with a kind smile. 'Who knows what he's after - but this is Colin we're talking about. I can guarantee he's got some yucky little plan up his sleeve – and he knows you're too…'

'Sappy?' I sigh.

'Kind!' insists Linda. 'He knows you're too kind to just cut him out of your life completely – even if that's what he deserves.'

I decide to gloss over that bit… though the idea of him having some kind of plan makes me squirm in my seat.

'Nah!' I shake my head at last and take a fortifying sip of coffee. 'I don't think he's up to anything. He was just drunk-dialling and being a bit of a prat, that's all. He's probably just a bit sad… I mean, it's coming up to Christmas… and it's the first one we've been apart. Officially, at least.'

'Whose fault's that?!' she splutters. 'I've seen the chaos that little weasel caused. Frankly - this sounds suspiciously like the last time he turned up out of the blue and you just let him straight back into your life.'

I flinch… mainly because she's right. That was back in the spring. He begged me for a second (or third… or fourth?) chance, and I simply didn't have the energy to say no.

'Be fair,' I say, my guts squeezing, 'we weren't *officially* separated then.'

'You'd started divorce proceedings!' she says, and I can hear the exasperation in her voice.

I get it... though I'm not going to admit that right now. Taking Colin back was a spectacularly poor choice... the man was a rubbish husband and simply incapable of keeping his candy cane in his pants. But... when he came crawling back, I was still reeling from losing Gramps. Who makes good choices when their entire life has imploded, anyway?

'It was just a rough patch,' I mutter, snapping the head off my Santa biscuit.

'Very rough,' says Linda. 'Considering he'd already left you for Marcia twice... or was it three times?'

'I don't know,' I mutter, grinding gingerbread into dust. 'I lost count. Anyway – can we change the subject? He's in the past... and it's nearly Christmas.'

I don't know why I keep saying that. It's like it's some kind of talisman or something... because *everything* works out at Christmas, doesn't it?! Or... it *should* do. We'll just ignore what happened last year!

'You'd better not be getting ready to forgive him again,' says Linda. 'That's all I'm saying.'

'Are you kidding me?' I splutter. I thought my friend knew me better than that. To be fair to her though... I *have* set a bit of a precedent.

'Hols... it's that time of year again,' says Linda.

'I took him back in the *spring*!' I huff. 'And it only lasted about two weeks.'

'Yeah – because he re-cheated on you with the same floozy!' Linda mutters darkly.

'I won't make that mistake again,' I say, my voice flat.

'But it's Christmas. You know what you're like… you go all… squishy!' laughs Linda.

'Yeah… well… not about him!' I say. 'Not anymore.'

"JINGLE BELLS! JINGLE BELLS! JINGLE ALL THE WAYYYYYY!"

We both stop talking long enough to belt out the line at the top of our lungs, earning ourselves a round of nervous giggles from the school kids piled in around the table behind us.

'You know… I've never been able to remember the rest of the words to that one!' laughs Linda.

'You and the rest of the world!' I say, nibbling my Santa biscuit, glad of the change of subject.

'Look… I promise to stop going on at you… but one more thing!' says Linda, picking up her headband and waving it at me so that the mistletoe dances up and down on the end of its spring.

'Don't you waggle your mistletoe at me, young lady!' I smirk.

Linda seems to miss the comedy value of the situation though, because she's got me pinned to my chair with a frown.

'Okay, what?' I demand when she's gone without blinking for far longer than I'm sure is good for her.

'Will you do me a favour?' she says, without a hint of a smile.

'Anything!' I say with an easy shrug.

'Good,' she says. 'Get the locks on your cottage changed.'

'Give over!' I laugh. 'That's total overkill.'

'It's really not,' she says. 'This is Colin we're talking about here. You should have done it ages ago. He's let himself in before, hasn't he?'

'Only because he left something behind,' I say, staring down into my coffee and avoiding her eye for all I'm worth. There's no way I'm telling her about the boxes in the attic.

'Uh huh?' says Linda, raising an eyebrow at me. 'Like what?'

'Just some of his clothes and bits and pieces,' I shrug. I really don't want to go there right now – Linda will do her nut if I tell her... and I haven't got the energy to deal with that after all that sherry.

It was after that little blip in the spring when I'd taken him back. According to Colin, he'd left some of his favourite shirts behind... but when I got back from work, I had the feeling he'd been fiddling around with more than just the contents of the wardrobe. I couldn't quite put my finger on it – but there were papers out of place on my desk in the study, and I could swear he'd gone through the drawers. What he was looking for is anyone's guess!

Anyway – that was months ago now, and nothing came of it. Maybe I was just being paranoid.

'Hols… I love you – but I'm serious,' says Linda, grabbing my hand.

'Fine!' I sigh. 'I'll do it just to keep you happy! I mean, it's not exactly on my list of fun festive things to do… but… I guess you're right!'

'I'm right if you don't want your idiot of an ex-husband ruining Christmas by turning up at your place, pissed out of his skull and ready to demand… well… who knows what!' she says, letting go of my hand again and shoving the rest of her Santa biscuit into her gob. 'This is Colin, remember - one of the world's biggest… biggest…'

Linda pauses, chewing quickly and clicking her fingers, clearly searching for the perfect word.

'Chocolate logs?' I suggest.

'That works!' she snorts. 'Though he's far less tasty.'

'Okay,' I sigh. 'You're right… I'll try to find someone, though I can't imagine it's going to be particularly easy this close to Christmas.'

Linda shrugs. 'There's got to be someone, hasn't there? I mean-'

'BRIGHTLY SHONE THE MOON AT NIGHT, THOUGH THE FROST WAS CROOOOOO-EEEELLLL!'

We both yell the line at the top of our lungs – as is our custom. This time, we manage to make Suze jump as she heads past us with a tray piled high with empties.

'You two are lucky you're my favourites!' she gasps, shooting a glare in our direction. 'I swear I'd chuck you out otherwise.'

'You wouldn't dream of it,' says Linda, pulling on her mistletoe headband and winking at her. 'We add to the ambience - now give us a kiss.'

'Get away with you!' chuckles Suze, rolling her eyes and heading towards the counter at speed.

'And you,' says Linda, turning back to me with a stern look – which is completely ruined by the mistletoe bouncing up and down in front of her forehead. 'I'm serious. I want you to do it today!'

'Okay, fine, I'll try,' I say, grabbing my phone and tapping out a few words. 'See?' I wave it in her face. 'It's officially on my to-do list.'

'Good!' says Linda, peering at me over the rim of her cup for a long moment. 'Because after everything King Scrooge of the North has thrown at you, you deserve a break!'

CHAPTER FOUR

EMBRACE YOUR ANGER - TURKEY'S A BIT BLAND WITHOUT SOME SEASONING

*a*s I head towards the lovely old brick building that holds Billingham's Finest Chocolates, I'm buzzing with an overload of caffeine and sugar.

I'm determined that today is going to be a *good* day. After all – I *do* own a chocolate factory and it *is* nearly Christmas. No amount of fretting over almost-ex-husbands or disgruntled Angels is going to bring me down today. Plus – I've got my first Christmas present to open! Linda remembered it just as we were saying our goodbyes and suggested I save it until I needed a giggle.

'Morning, Gramps,' I whisper as I pause for a moment to smile up at Billingham's. My breath steams in the chilly air – I think it's even colder now than when I set out from home – but I can't resist my little morning ritual. Gramps has been gone for more than a year now, but every time I stand here, looking up at the factory, it's like he's right beside me.

Billingham's is a lovely place, though it's not *technically* a factory anymore. Back when I was really little – the huge kitchens at the back of the building were still in full swing - emitting the most glorious, chocolatey smells as Gramps's team dreamed up new treats. The kitchens have been closed for several decades now. We source our chocolate from all over the world and we've got a reputation for curating the most delicious collections from the best chocolatiers... but the original Billingham's magic? That started in our own kitchens.

Gramps founded Billingham's Finest Chocolates in his twenties... so it's been going a seriously long time. I spent a great deal of my childhood snuggled between its walls. There was nothing better than coming to work with Gramps and being petted by his adoring workforce. I just wish I still had that easy relationship with the Angels these days.

Things were fine when I officially joined Billingham's early last summer to start up social media accounts for the company – in fact, Doris and co love nothing more than giggling their way through videos for their adoring fans - but I guess things were bound to change when we lost Gramps and I took over as "boss".

Gramps never officially retired. He always said he loved his work too much – so he just kept going, right into his eighties. I know it shouldn't have been a shock when he got sick at the end of last summer... but I think it took us all by surprise. He ended up in hospital with a chest infection - and simply never came home. As his right-hand woman, Doris stepped up and kept everything running at the factory while he was in hospital... but to be fair to Gramps, the man was still placing orders and coming up with new ideas for Billingham's right up until his final breath.

Then we lost him – and as per his wishes – I became Managing Director of the whole caboodle. Of course, I was still with Colin then, and boy did he have a lot to say on the subject. We hadn't even held the funeral before he started to badger me about leaving Billingham's. He wanted me to sell the business – or even better, scrap it and sell the building to developers.

I was in bits – something that definitely wasn't helped by his relentless pestering about what we could do with the money if I "stopped being so selfish". According to him, holding on to the factory and all my memories of Gramps was just self-indulgent. I think that's when I knew it was only a matter of time before our marriage fell apart.

Of course - in the end, we didn't so much *fall apart* as go full neutron-star-implosion. Ah – the joys of last Christmas! Anyway, I've spent most of this year doing my best to escape the gravitational pull of the resulting black hole.

I suck in a deep, slightly shaky breath. Didn't I

promise myself I wasn't going to do this today? I need to get on with it and go inside.

'Come on Holly!' I mutter, plastering a smile back on my face. 'It's nearly Christmas!'

My smile instantly relaxes and becomes real as I step beneath the heavy Christmas garland that's been draped above the factory entrance. Billingham's has always done Christmas properly, and Alf's Angels aren't about to let the side down just because the man himself is no longer around to keep tabs.

As I reach the main packing floor, I come to a standstill and stare around. It might be early - but it looks like I'm the last one here. A spear of guilt hits me in the chest as I watch everyone beavering away, consulting lists and packing our distinctive holiday hampers.

Alf's Angels might be well past retirement age, but it doesn't slow them down in the slightest. The air is thick with cheerful chatter as the life-long friends work steadily to fulfil our Christmas orders. With just a few days before the last post, the factory floor is about as hectic as it gets.

Even with our great loss still hanging over us, it's been a busy year at Billingham's. We've found a whole new swathe of fans through our social media channels, the orders have been flooding in and it looks like we might even sell out of some favourites before the big day. Thankfully, the Angels have got it all in hand... even if I haven't!

Every single day here at Billingham's is bittersweet and I still can't believe the place is mine. It's taking me ages to wrap my head around it… in fact, I'm not sure I ever will. I've not changed much at all since I took over. The Angels still rule the roost and I still feel like I'm just "boss" on paper.

I *have* found a bit of a workaround to this though - I basically pretend I'm not in charge and defer to Doris for everything. She was always Gramps's right-hand-woman. She kept the place going when he was ill – and she's still doing it now – more than a year later.

I watch Doris for a moment, scribbling away in the ancient ledger where she records every order that comes in. I've done my best to convert her to a laptop – but she's having none of it.

I turn to watch the others again – packing every order by hand with so much care and attention. There's a general resistance to change here… but I'm learning it's something to embrace rather than something to fight against. Our old-fashioned vibe and values are what set Billingham's apart. The Angels are tireless in their pursuit of perfection – and the fact that we're basically staffed by a bunch of grandmas and great-aunts seems to delight new fans and long-standing customers alike.

'Morning, Holly,' says Doris, appearing as if by magic at my side and thrusting a Billingham's mug in my direction. She might be miffed with me for some reason, but she always had a drink ready for Gramps in the morning - and Doris isn't the kind of woman to let some mysterious, unspoken grudge get in the way of tradition.

'Morning!' I say, shooting her a grateful smile as I take the mug. 'Sorry I'm late... or... not as early as you lot!'

I glance up at the huge old carriage clock on the wall just to make sure I haven't made a mistake. Sure enough – I'm here with at least twenty minutes to spare before the official start of the day – just as I planned. By the looks of things though, the rest of them have been hard at it for at least an hour already.

'It's fine,' says Doris. 'It's your morning for coffee with Linda, isn't it?'

I nod, wondering how she remembers all these little details.

'That's why I made you a mint tea,' she says, pointing at the mug. 'You've probably had more than enough coffee to last you until New Year!'

'Ta!' I say, doing my best not to feel like a naughty kid being told off for eating too many sweets. I pull myself up, trying to remember what Linda said about being the boss. 'Anything to report? Anything I need to deal with?'

'Everything's on time and on schedule,' says Doris, shaking her head. 'Nothing to report. No problems and no one's off ill.'

I can't help but smile at that. No one at Billingham's is ever off ill... or at least that's what it feels like.

Considering the average age of our workforce is some-where around seventy-five, it's a bit of a miracle really. But then, Billingham's *is* a wonderful place to work. Everyone seems to love nothing more than spending their days here... and I don't think it hurts that the place smells of chocolate and there's always a plentiful supply of tea and biscuits on tap.

'I'm glad everyone's okay,' I say. 'Not long until Christmas.'

'Not long,' Doris agrees with a nod.

I can practically feel the ice crystals forming between us. I can't exactly blame Doris though – I've known her all my life, but here *I* am sounding like festive-bot. I just wish I knew how to break down this weird wall that's formed between us. Even more – I wish I knew what put it there in the first place!

'Right... so... I'll be in the office if anyone needs me,' I say.

'Right you are,' says Doris.

Letting out a little sigh, I carry my mint tea towards the office at the back of the building, smiling and nodding at everyone as I edge between the various packing tables with their posh boxes, rolls of fancy wrapping paper and ribbons.

I pause briefly next to Iris Bennet's desk. I can't resist. Iris has been with Billingham's since the begin-ning – she's an original Angel - and I swear there's some kind of magic at work whenever she's got her calligraphy pen in her hand.

'Okay there, Holly?' she asks, glancing up briefly.

I smile and nod. She just shrugs and goes back to what she's doing – though this isn't unusual for Iris – she's a woman of very few words at the best of times. Still – she's a genius, and I linger a bit longer just to catch a glimpse of her pen in action.

Iris hand-writes all our cards – order cards, Christmas cards and little notes. Some of our long-standing regulars get a full-blown, gossipy letter with their order… but that's what makes us so unique. Billingham's has always treated our customers as close friends… and that's pretty rare these days!

Today, Iris is busy working away with emerald-green ink, and I can't help but stare as the letters glisten in the wake of her pen. For several long minutes, I stand, mesmerised, until Iris pauses and clears her throat. She glances up at me with a worried look on her face.

'Sorry,' I say quickly, shaking my head as the spell is broken. 'I'll just…' I trail off and shoot her a quick smile before turning to let myself quietly into my office.

CHAPTER FIVE

IF LIFE HANDS YOU A LUMP OF COAL,
BUILD AN ANGRY SNOWMAN

*C*losing the door softly behind me, I have to resist the urge to slump back against the glass. That wouldn't do at all. As much as that was supremely awkward - it's nearly Christmas and the Angels are run off their feet. There's no way I want to jeopardise things with any kind of dramatics!

Still… I think I have to face the fact that whatever's going on isn't going to miraculously solve itself. I've been cherishing a vague hope that everything might blow over by Christmas but…

'Too much to ask,' I sigh.

Heading over towards the desk, I flop down into my chair and fire up the laptop. I need to find a locksmith – and there's no time like the present. Thanks to Linda, I've gone from blissfully ignoring the situation to feeling more than a little bit panicky about the whole thing. The last thing I want is to come downstairs on Christmas morning, only to find Colin in my kitchen!

Still… changing the locks feels like a supremely stroppy thing to do – it's really not my style at all. If I had my way, the divorce would be over and done with – preferably without any fuss. I just want to forget about the entire thing and move on with my life.

As I wait for the computer to run through several updates, I grab the gift Linda gave me from my handbag. If ever there was a moment for a good giggle – it's right now.

I turn the gold package over in my hands a few times, admiring Linda's neat wrapping. If I didn't know my best friend better, I'd hazard a guess at this being a book… but that doesn't seem very likely, somehow! Rude willy-shaped toys wearing Christmas clothing are more her style (based on last year's gift anyway!) I shrug and tear into the paper. Sure enough, out falls a glossy, hardback book.

'How to Be Angry At Christmas! By S Claus'

I grin and roll my eyes. Linda's always on at me for being too soft. She reckons if I could just muster the courage to lose my rag a bit more often, I'd be happier. I mean… talk about contradictory advice! Flipping through the pages, I choose one at random.

"If life hands you a lump of coal, build an angry snowman."

'Really useful!' I giggle, rolling my eyes. Well… she was right. It *did* make me laugh, even if it's not exactly going to solve any of life's big issues!

I push the book out of the way and grab my notepad instead. It's time to start rummaging around online for local locksmiths!

'Please let this be easy!' I mutter, pulling up a search engine.

It only takes a couple of minutes to gather a list of likely suspects, and I stare down at the phone numbers for a long moment. I really don't want to do this!

Glancing around for a distraction, I shoot a longing look at the basket full of post that's been left for me to open. It looks like it's mostly Christmas cards… I *adore* opening cards. It's definitely a more appealing job than finding someone to Colin-proof the cottage for me before Christmas!

'I know, I'll alternate it!' I say, grabbing the pile of festive-looking post and arranging it into a neat stack in front of me. Now… where to start – card or call first?

'Card first!' I say like the princess of procrastination I am.

Picking up Gramps's old-fashioned letter-opener, I slit open the first envelope and draw out a card. The cute robin instantly brings a smile to my face. Flipping it open, I read the friendly little note inside. It's from one of our suppliers in Belgium. They make the creamiest, most delicious truffles I've ever tasted – they were one of Gramps's many favourites. This year, their bumper Christmas delivery included a huge hamper of goodies for us all to share.

'You can go there!' I say, tucking the card onto the string looped across the chalkboard on the wall behind my desk. My office is already practically lined with cards… I've nearly run out of space.

Right, I guess it's time to call the first number on my list.

Pouting mightily, I grab the receiver from the old-fashioned Bakelite rotary phone and dial before I can think better of it.

'Hi. You've reached Lock, Stock and Key. We're closed until the fifth of January. If you want to book a slot for next year, leave a message and we'll call you then. Merry Christmas!'

I sigh and put the phone down. Then, grabbing my pen, I draw a line through the first number on the pad.

Ten minutes later, I have a teetering pile of empty envelopes stacked up in front of me, and it's becoming practically impossible to find spaces to hang the new cards.

Mind you - Christmas card placement is the least of my worries right now. I'm nearing the end of my list of phone numbers, and so far I've only succeeded in leaving a lot of answering machine messages. Something's telling me I won't be hearing back from anyone this side of singing Auld Lang Syne!

I let out a long sigh and pick up the last piece of post. The green envelope feels bulky and expensive, and there's a logo embossed across the back.

Curves.

Isn't that some fancy-pants marketing company?

I turn it over to check out the address and let out a groan. Well… this one *definitely* isn't going to cheer me up, is it?

'Colin Sloan - Managing Director?' I splutter. 'In his dreams!'

It looks like everything about today is conspiring to ram my ex down my throat - no matter how desperate I am to put him out of my mind – and my life! The question is – why is Colin receiving post here at Billingham's? Not only is he most definitely *not* the Managing Director – he's never even worked at the factory!

I don't bother with the posh letter opener this time – I rip into the envelope without ceremony and yank out the contents. There's a Christmas card, and as soon as I open it a smaller, heavy black envelope falls out onto the desk. So *that's* why the thing was so bulky!

Flipping the card open, I scan the words inside with a frown.

"Colin. More logos for your consideration - printed up as promised.

Invoice has been forwarded and payment now overdue.
We're looking forward to hearing from you shortly."

Feeling slightly sick, I reach for the little black packet and tear it open. Several chunky business cards scatter across my desk

'What the actual…?'

I scan them and feel any festive spirit I still had going on swirl and disappear down some kind of cosmic plughole. The cards all bear the same name - "Colin Sloan - Managing Director", but as I flip them over, I notice they've got various different logos.

Sloan and Billingham
Sloan's Finest Chocolates
Slone's Awesome Yummy Goodness

'Nope nope nope,' I growl.

I've got no idea what's going on right now, but there's only one place these monstrosities belong. Leaning down, I grab my waste paper basket from under the desk and sweep the entire lot into the bin, closely followed by the pile of envelopes. I'm just about to add the last Christmas card for good measure when I pause. It's seriously cute. A starry sky with a sleigh being drawn by mice. There's even a rabbit wearing a Santa hat.

There's no point wasting a perfectly good card, is there?

I turn to the already-stuffed wall behind my desk and shuffle the other cards along so that I can add the newcomer.

'There,' I say, forcing my voice to sound bright and breezy... as though something very weird isn't going on. 'Job done.'

Still ignoring the elephant in the room – namely the fact that my almost-ex-husband seems to be in the middle of some kind of rebrand for *my* company – I sit back down at the desk and stare at the remaining numbers scrawled on my notepad.

Is there even any point?

Glancing at my Christmas present from Linda sitting at the back of the desk, I straighten up. I promised... and considering my best friend is tenacious to the point of driving a girl to sherry... well, let's just say I'd better get on with it!

I'm just reaching for the receiver when the phone springs to life - its loud, musical trill making me jump so badly that my buttocks actually leave my seat.

'Please please please...!' I gasp. Maybe I'm in luck - maybe one of them has taken pity on my increasingly desperate messages and managed to fit me in!

'Billingham's Finest Chocolates - Holly speaking?' I say, forcing myself to sound as cheerful as possible.

'How about this, Miss bloody Billingham... how about you stop trying to steal my boyfriend behind my back?'

'Marcia?'

I have to resist the urge to face-palm. What on earth have I done to deserve this?

'Of course it's me - unless you're busy trying to wreck anyone else's relationship at the moment... though that wouldn't surprise me!'

I take a long, slow breath. There's no point rising to the bait.

'So – what have you got to say for yourself?' Marcia growls. 'Calling my boyfriend in the middle of the night and asking him over to your place...! I mean... did you think I wouldn't find out?'

I open my mouth to tell Marcia exactly what happened, but the woman has gone into auto-rant mode.

'Seriously – you're pathetic,' she spits. 'Colin told me everything – and he said you were very persuasive!'

I let out a kind of grunt. If I'm honest, I'm surprised Colin can remember anything about the phone call, given how drunk he sounded.

'Think it's funny, do you?' says Marcia. 'It's embarrassing! You're embarrassing! I mean... begging isn't a good look, you know. Plus - it's Christmas! Trying to steal someone else's bloke just before the big day... it's... it's... despic-balls-stical!'

I bite my lip to stop myself from laughing out loud. I'm pretty sure the word she's looking for might be *despicable* – or maybe *diabolical*?

Swallowing hard in an attempt to get rid of the rising

hysteria, I shake my head. Frankly, it's all a bit rich - considering it was just last Christmas I found Colin and Marcia in bed together... in my cottage! That in itself would have been bad enough – but they chose to do it on the day I went to lay a wreath on Gramps's grave. Colin refused to come with me and then... I came home to *that*.

I take a long, slow breath, willing the gruesome image away.

'You know,' I say, trying to sound as calm and polite as possible, 'I'm at work right now. Do you think we could talk about this later?'

Preferably never! It's not something I *ever* want to talk about. Linda knows the details... but she's the only one.

I close my eyes... just in case I have the ability to magically reset this weird day. If only I could rewind to last night when I was hanging my favourite baubles, then I could just ignore Colin's phone call - like I should have done in the first place.

'I know you want him back,' says Marcia.

My eyes snap open. Sadly, I'm still firmly in the middle of the mess.

'I can't believe you'd do that to another woman,' she huffs, 'I'm never talking to you again!'

I open my mouth to tell her that I'm already looking forward to the peace and quiet - when there's an almighty thump on the other end of the line, followed by a great deal of muffled swearing. I think Marcia just tried to slam the phone down on me and ended up dropping it instead.

Gently putting the phone down, I let my face slump into my hands. I'm already exhausted - and it's not even lunchtime.

Still… if Colin's up to his old tricks again, it probably means Linda's right. He's likely to try crawling back into my life again. This time… I'm not going to let that happen.

CHAPTER SIX

THEY SAY LAUGHTER IS THE BEST MEDICINE, BUT HAVE YOU TRIED A HEARTY SCREAM INTO A PILLOW? IT'S THE NEW YOGA

'No – I'm completely booked up.'

I let out a long breath. This is locksmith number three thousand, four hundred and fifty. Okay – so that might be a *slight* exaggeration… but still, I feel like I've been at this for hours.

'Oh!' I say.

'Should have booked me sooner,' he adds.

I bite my lip and nod, even though I know the guy at *We Three Keys* can't see me. Somehow I've got a feeling Linda would agree with him right now.

'You don't have any space for emergencies?' I ask.

I know, I know… Colin being a drunken pain in my chestnut stuffing is hardly an emergency, but Linda's dire warnings this morning have got my feathers well and truly ruffled.

'Sorry.' The guy sounds decidedly un-sorry. I can

practically hear the shrug in his voice. 'Try your local police station – they might be able to send someone.'

'Okay, thanks. I don't suppose-'

The line goes dead. I blow a raspberry at the receiver before plonking it back in its cradle. Right… well… that's that then. My entire list is officially exhausted. Unless…

Getting to my feet, I wander over to the little window that looks out on the factory floor.

I wonder...

I stare out at the dozen or so silver heads bent intently over their work. I might not be their favourite person right now – for reasons unfathomable - but I *am* technically their boss. It's got to be worth a quick ask, hasn't it? Alf's Angels seem to know everyone and everything that goes on around here. In fact, I could swear they run this town behind my back. Maybe one of them knows someone who might be able to help me out.

Doing my best to smooth out my slightly crumpled top, I head back out onto the factory floor. For a moment, I just stand and watch everyone at work.

Why is this so hard? I always used to feel so at home here, but these days I feel like a spare part… a total lemon… one that's going off and everyone's doing their best to avoid because it's gone all blue and hairy.

'Erm…' I say, trying to ignore the nerves that seem to have got a sudden grip on my voice box.

No one looks up. No one even notices I'm here.

I clear my throat and Doris glances at me from behind the huge hamper she's busy packing. Her hands still as she stares at me.

'I'd like to ask a quick question?' I say.

My voice is still far too quiet to carry over the gentle babble of Alf's Angels as they work. Their chatter combined with the rustling of fancy wrapping paper, the tying of silvery bows and the scratching of Iris's calligraphy nib creates a soothing festive lullaby. It used to make me feel so safe and happy... now, it just makes me feel a bit sad.

Doris gets to her feet, grabs a handbell from the counter nearby and gives it a hearty shake. The effect is instant. A dozen pairs of eyes swivel in her direction. She simply points at me and they all turn as one. Some of them look surprised to find me standing here.

'Thanks, Doris,' I say, shooting her a small smile.

Doris just nods, crossing her arms tightly and fixing me with a look. I wouldn't say it's *unfriendly...* but it isn't exactly warm and cuddly either!

'So... erm... hi!' I say. 'I won't keep you a sec - but I was just wondering if anyone knows a... um... a lock-smith?' I pause 'It's... well... I guess it's a bit urgent. I've called everyone I can find online, but they're either booked up or finished for Christmas.'

I stop, feeling more like a six-year-old asking for pocket money than the Managing Director of a successful company. The stony looks the Angels are now throwing my way really aren't helping matters either. Anyone would think I've just insulted each of them individually…and then followed up with all their relations just for good measure.

I force myself to look from woman to woman, but most of them won't meet my eye. The ones that do give me a good glare.

Okay… so this isn't *quite* the reaction I was hoping for. I mean… I wasn't expecting any of them to magic a solution out of thin air, and I know it was a bit of a long shot… but I really wasn't prepared for open hostility!

'Is this… for the factory?' says Doris, her voice rumbling at me like an unspent thunderstorm.

'Billingham's?' I say in surprise.

Why on earth would I be changing the locks here?

I frown as I look between the Angels again… and they all stare stonily back at me. There are some seriously crossed wires going on here somewhere.

I take a deep breath. I'd quite like to scuttle back to my office right now, but that would just be daft. There's only one way to go with this – the complete truth. Sure – it's my personal life we're talking about here - but the Angels have always been like a gaggle of extra grandmas… or at least they used to be.

'No,' I say, making sure they can all hear me. 'Not for Billingham's. It's for the cottage. My cottage. I know I've left it until the last minute - but I'm really hoping to get the locks changed before Christmas.'

I pause to let a low wave of surprised muttering subside.

'I thought it might be a good idea… you know…' I pause again feeling slightly awkward. This is my work-force… my employees. I don't owe them any kind of explanation. But – they've watched me grow up, and I *think* they still care. Deep down. 'You know,' I repeat, 'with the divorce almost finalised, and Colin… being Colin.'

I know it's a bit of a lame finish, but as much as I want to be honest with them, they really don't need to know all the sordid ins and outs of Colin's betrayal. It's bad enough that I already hate myself for taking him back after what he did… I don't need the same kind of judgment from them!

There's a low rumble as the Angels turn to each other. Mutters and shrugs abound… but no offer of any kind of a solution.

'Ah well,' I say, forcing myself to give an easy shrug even though I'm starting to feel pretty daft. 'Not to worry – I just thought I'd ask!'

Unable to face the collective gaze of the Angels any longer, I duck my head and retreat to the relative safety of my office, closing the door behind me. After a couple of deep breaths, I cast a quick glance out of the window.

Great!

It looks like there's some kind of unofficial meeting well and truly underway out there. Everyone's gathered around Doris and judging by the amount of arm waving and enthusiastic hand gestures in the direction of the office, I'm assuming I'm the hot topic of conversation right now.

Doing my best to draw some kind of comfort from the cosy, glittering lamplight of Gramps's office – *my* office – I head back towards my desk. All I want is to enjoy Christmas – is that too much to ask?!

A soft knock on the door makes me halt in my tracks. I blink hard, willing away the frustrated tears that are threatening to spill over. They've got nothing to do with Colin – I don't want him back - but I *would* like to reclaim the happy, carefree excitement this time of year always used to bring with it. Christmas has always been my favourite. I don't want it to become a permanent casualty of my ill-feted marriage to Grinchy-Mc-Grinchface!

'Hello?' I call, wishing I could just go home and hang out next to my gorgeous twinkly tree.

The door cracks open and Iris's face appears. 'Can I come in?'

'Of course!' I say in surprise.

Iris steps quietly inside, leaning on her flowery walking stick, and closes the door behind her.

'This is for you,' she says, holding out a notecard.

'Erm - thanks?' I say, taking it on autopilot. There, in Iris's elegant calligraphy, is a name and telephone number. 'Who's Steve?' I say.

I feel like I've just turned two pages in a book and missed a vital plot point.

'My nephew,' says Iris with a small smile. 'Actually – my great nephew. He'll be able to help you out. Any trouble, just tell him his Aunty Iris told you to call him and that he's to do as he's told.'

Before I can say another word, Iris has already left the office and is beetling back towards her desk. I can hear her cane tip-tapping as she goes.

I hurry over to the door and lean out.

'Thank you!' I call after her, not wanting to let the moment pass without making sure she knows I appreciate her help.

Iris smiles at me as she settles herself back at her desk. I watch for a moment as she pops her glasses back on her nose, shifts the ancient angle-poise lamp into a better position, and gets straight back to work with her delicate nib pen.

I'm just about to force myself to look away before I get hypnotised by the flow of ink again when I feel someone's eyes on me. Turning on the spot, I find Doris watching me closely. I shoot an uncertain smile in her direction and she returns it, giving me a little thumbs up. The simple gesture makes me well up again and I practically melt with gratitude. It's just so... familiar. Friendly... unassuming... and everything that's been missing for months.

'Get a grip, Holly!' I mutter as I scuttle back into the office, blinking hard. See... this is what comes from staying up late to play with tinsel and a little bit too much sherry. I'm an emotional disaster zone!

Giving myself a moment to get it together, I take a deep breath and pick up the phone for the umpteenth time this morning. It's time to give the mythical Steve a call.

The phone seems to ring for an eternity. I'll give it four more rings…

Or maybe ten…

It goes to answer machine and I hang up without leaving a message. But… I refuse to give up. I dial again and cross my fingers. This time, I'll leave a message. After all – Steve's my last hope!

'What?!'

I widen my eyes as the curt answer takes me by surprise. *Charming!*

'Erm hi… my name's Holly? I need to change the front door lock on my cottage…?'

Everything's coming out as a question – but mainly because I'm not entirely sure if he's still there. I pause for a beat, but he doesn't say a word.

'It'd be great if there's any chance I can get it done before Christmas.' I pause again. 'Look… I know it's really last minute.'

I'm pretty sure I can hear breathing on the other end of the line… but he still doesn't say anything. If this guy wasn't Iris's nephew, I think I'd be putting the phone down right about now!

Maybe it's time to deploy the magic words. 'Your Aunty Iris said I should give you a call.'

'Wait,' comes the gruff voice at long last. 'What did you say your name was?'

'Holly,' I say. 'Holly Billingham.'

'As in… Alf's granddaughter?' he says.

Something's just changed… but I'm not sure what!

'Yeah. That's me,' I say.

'Right. Sorry,' he says quickly. 'Of course I can come over and take a look… when's good for you?'

CHAPTER SEVEN

IN THE GRAND MASTERPIECE OF LIFE,
ANGER IS JUST A BOLD BRUSHSTROKE.
MAKE YOURS PICASSO-WORTHY - JUST
AVOID SPLATTERING TOO MANY PEOPLE

Steve Marshall arrives right on time. That fact alone surprises the living daylights out of me. I guess I'm just too used to Colin's timekeeping which is… well… rude. There's no other word for it.

I've been standing at the living room window for a good ten minutes - half admiring my lovely tree, and half keeping a decidedly sceptical eye on the driveway. I have to admit – a big part of me wasn't expecting him to show up at all - let alone on time!

Dashing for the front door, I send Steve a silent apology for being so cynical. Let's face it though, he's basically reached mythical-beast status just by turning up on time.

At least it's still light outside. I have to admit, it feels pretty strange to be home in the middle of the afternoon waiting for a random stranger to turn up at the cottage, but Steve mentioned that it'd be a much simpler job to do in the daylight. The minute I got off the phone, I pulled on my big-girl pants and had a word with Doris. She was unexpectedly easy-going about the whole thing and was more than happy to lock up for me – especially when I told her why I needed to head home early. In fact, she practically frog-marched me to the factory door!

I plaster a smile on my face as I open the front door. There's a little white van parked up on my driveway just the other side of the garden gate. There's no sign of Steve, but I guess he must be getting his tools out of the back.

Glancing around in a bid to ignore the random swoop of nerves in my stomach, I spot Eileen's curtains twitching next door. I can't help but grin – my neighbour likes to keep an eye on who's coming and going. She's not used to me being at home during the day either! I wave at her window – just in case she's looking this way through the net curtains.

'Hi!'

The greeting makes me turn back towards the gate, and I almost laugh out loud. Steve's basically a huge smile beneath an enormous, fluffy bobble hat. He's got it pulled down so low that I can't make out much of his face, but at least he looks nothing like the total grouch I was expecting!

'Holly?'

I nod dumbly.

'Oh good! I always get the roads around here mixed up.'

I smile and nod again. Then I clear my throat... it's time to actually say words - any words - before he thinks I'm a complete imbecile!

'Very twisty,' I say.

'Huh?' says Steve, that smile getting even wider.

'The roads!' I say, trying to clarify my random statement. 'Would you like to come in?' I add, doing my best to be normal for all of five seconds.

'Thanks, I will,' Steve nods, 'but first... I need to beg a favour.'

Uh oh!

'It's nothing major!' he laughs.

Gah - now I'm blushing. He has a ridiculously nice laugh. It makes me think of hot chocolate with a splash of Baileys... or a warm blanket after a long walk in the snow... or the smell of the tree on Christmas morning...

The blush has just turned supernova – and I've got the feeling I'm turning a very fetching shade of beetroot here! I don't need to look in a mirror to verify it either... I can practically feel the steam rising out of the top of my head.

'Holly – are you okay?' he says.

That smile of his is wavering and he sounds worried. I can't exactly blame him – I'm guessing I look more than a little bit deranged! I quickly nod, trying not to wonder too hard about whether he's as cute as his laugh makes him sound. It's impossible to tell under that hat!

'You said you needed a favour?' I prompt, hoping to deflect his attention away from the fact I'm making a total idiot of myself.

'Right... yeah. I've got my dog with me,' he says. 'He's old and he doesn't like being left in the van on his own... and I *really* don't like leaving him in there when it's so cold. I was wondering if I could bring him inside?'

'Oh!' I say. 'Well...'

A dog? I love dogs. Why am I being such an idiot? The truth is - there's something about this guy that has me on the hop!

'He's very polite,' adds Steve.

'Of course - bring him in!' I say, giving myself a shake.

Pull it together, woman!

Steve shoots me a grateful smile and heads back towards the passenger side of the van. Two seconds later, he's making his way up the garden path with the most gorgeous old dog plodding along behind him.

'Holly, this is Arthur - Arthur, Holly.'

Arthur stares up at me with liquid brown eyes and something inside me melts. He's a huge chocolate Labrador, but the fur around his muzzle is speckled with grey. He's also wearing a very snazzy red and white jumper with little holly leaves all over it.

'I like your jumper! I croon.

'Blame Aunty Iris,' chuckles Steve. 'He's got a whole collection!'

I grin down at Arthur, doing my best to rein in the urge to drop to my knees and scoop this beautiful, furry old guy up into a hug. Instead, I hold my hand out for him to sniff. He promptly gives me a lick and wags his tail a couple of times.

'Oh good!' says Steve. 'Looks like you two are going to get along just fine!'

'Come on in, Arthur,' I say. 'Oh… and you too I guess!' I add, smiling over my shoulder at Steve. The old dog potters straight past me and heads into the hallway. I watch as he turns in three little circles on the spot and then makes himself comfortable on a patch of carpet.

'Well – that's him well and truly at home already then!' laughs Steve, popping his toolbox down on the front doorstep. 'I'd better have a look at this lock while we've still got some light out here.'

I'm impressed… it doesn't look like I'm going to have to do much chivvying with this one! I watch as he bends to inspect the latch.

'Perfect,' he says with a satisfied nod before rummaging around in his toolbox and pulling out a cardboard package. 'I had this at home – it's left over from another job – but it should fit nicely without too much jiggery-pokery. I can get on with it now – as long as that's okay with you?'

'Fab – yes please!' I say, slightly distracted by the

sight of Arthur, who's busy washing his front paws and looking ridiculously cute.

'Actually... while I've got you here - I wanted to apologise,' says Steve, taking his hat off and running his fingers through a crop of wavy, shiny hair the colour of caramel.

Ah, crap... did he really have to look *this* good?

Unable to tear my eyes off him, I feel myself crumple up inside. I've just spent the last five minutes acting like a complete moron in front of one of the most beautiful men I've ever seen in my life!

Focus, Holly! You can save the situation... maybe!

If I can just act like a mildly-sane human being for the next few minutes... maybe he won't think I'm a complete knob.

'You were saying?' I prompt, willing myself not to disappear into a daydream that involves me, Steve and a long, soapy bubble bath. 'You want to apologise? For what?!'

'The way I answered the phone earlier!' he says, searching around in his toolbox again and lining up a couple of tools on the doormat, ready for action. 'I must have sounded so rude - but I was up a ladder when you called, putting up decorations for Mr Ericson - my elderly neighbour. Then Arthur decided to have a snooze right at the bottom - and I nearly trampled him on the way down.'

I grin at him. So, it's not just me having one of *those* days then!

'It's fine!' I laugh. 'I'm just really grateful that you're here at all!'

'It's my pleasure,' says Steve. 'I was hoping I'd have something to fit your door, but if not - I could have nipped into town and fitted it for you tomorrow instead. Or… you know… whenever was convenient!'

'Blimey,' I laugh, 'do all your annoying, last-minute customers get this kind of service?!'

Steve looks up at me, pausing in the act of yanking the cardboard packaging away from the new lock. I feel something warm slide into my belly like I've just swallowed a spoonful of cinnamon honey. Oh man, those eyes could be my undoing in a heartbeat!

'They definitely don't,' he rumbles, shooting me a smile that makes me shiver. 'But, you're Alf Billingham's granddaughter, you're Aunty Iris's boss, and frankly - anyone who keeps her on, doing a job that she loves…'

He pauses and glances down at his hands for a moment.

'Billingham's means the world to Iris,' he says slowly. 'And - by extension - to me too. I'd have done pretty much anything for Alf… and now – the same goes for you, Holly.'

CHAPTER EIGHT

ANGER IS JUST YOUR INNER SUPERHERO
GETTING READY FOR BATTLE

I fidget as Steve inspects the door again and then grabs a screwdriver. If I'm honest, I'm not sure what to do with myself. I really want to stay and watch what he's up to - but Colin always hated it when I did that.

Mind you, that was different – it was a necessity. Colin needed watching closely unless I wanted him drilling through the mains electricty cable... or hammering a nail through a water pipe.

'Erm... would you like a drink?' I say, watching as he makes quick work of sliding the old lock out of place.

'Nah, I'm good thanks,' he says, shooting me a grateful smile.

'Oh, okay,' I mumble. Damn - at least it would have given me something to do. 'Do you mind if I stay and watch what you're up to?'

'Of course not!' he laughs. 'Why would I?'

I shrug. Colin's already taking up far too much space in my own head... I don't think I want to start whinging on about him to this unexpectedly hot visitor.

Steve grabs a chisel and starts shaving curls of wood away from the edges of the hole.

'This won't take long – and it should be far more secure than the old one,' he says. 'So... I'm guessing the fact I'm here means that your husband is finally out of the picture?'

My eyebrows fly up and I gape at him. That was... *weirdly* personal. But then, I guess I *have* called him out to a supposed emergency. So much for keeping Colin out of the conversation, though.

'I'm sorry!' he says, glancing in my direction. 'I didn't mean to be rude... it's just that Aunty Iris keeps me up to date with everything that's going on at Billingham's.'

'Oh... she does?'

I mean that's fair enough... but the spectacular car crash of my marriage is *hardly* work-related!

'Please - don't take it the wrong way!' he says quickly. 'It's just that the factory is the most important thing in her life - it's natural she talks about it so much.'

'I suppose...' I say, nodding slowly.

'Seriously Holly,' he says, 'Aunty Iris thinks of you more as a surrogate granddaughter. I think all the Angels do!'

'I'm not sure about that!' I laugh, doing my best not to sound bitter. 'Actually, I'm not sure any of them are that keen on me right now... though I've got no idea what I'm meant to have done wrong. I guess I'm not Gramps - and that's enough in itself.'

Steve places the chisel down and turns to face me properly. I instantly feel glued to the spot. He's not smiling anymore – and those hazel eyes seem to hold a flicker of fire I don't quite understand.

I shift uncomfortably. This conversation is getting weirder by the second. I can't believe I just said that to a complete stranger - even if he is Iris's nephew. I only just met the guy!

'What?!' I demand, my spine stiffening slightly.

'It's not about your Gramps,' he says, not taking his eyes off me.

'What then?' I say.

'They're all just worried, Holly,' he says. 'Surely you can understand that?'

'But... why?' I say. 'What about?'

'About their jobs,' he says, and I get the sense he's struggling not to add "duh!" to the end of the sentence.

'But... why?' I say again. 'Billingham's isn't going anywhere!'

He gives me a piercing look – and I feel a bit like he's trying to catch me out in a lie.

'What?!' I demand, my hackles rising. 'It's not! Just because we lost Gramps, it doesn't mean the company is going the same way. That's why he made me

Managing Director – so that everything would carry on without interruption.'

'But… you're going through a divorce, right?' he says gently.

'That's got nothing to do with it,' I huff.

'I'm afraid that's not what your ex told everyone,' he says quietly.

My head suddenly feels like it's about to explode, and I take a step back. Arthur, clearly sensing there's something wrong, hauls himself to his feet - but rather than making a beeline for Steve like I expect him to, he comes to me and leans his heavy head against my leg.

'I'm sorry - I didn't mean to upset you!' says Steve quickly.

'You didn't,' I say, my voice tight.

'That's not what Arthur's telling me right now!' he says.

I look down at the dog and stroke his silky ears.

'Fine. I'm upset!' I say. 'Colin hasn't got anything to do with Billingham's. He doesn't work there and he never has. Why would he be telling the Angels anything?'

'Because-' he starts. 'Actually, never mind.'

'Oh come on!' I huff. 'You can't just stop now. Tell me what's really going on.'

'Maybe just ask Iris and the others?' he says, looking decidedly shifty and clearly wishing we hadn't strayed onto this topic.

'Trust me, I will,' I say. 'But at least give me some

idea of what I'm going to be walking into. Things have been off for ages!'

'Fine,' he says, holding his hands up in surrender. 'But I'm really not the best person to talk to about this.'

'Well tough!' I say, marvelling at just how grouchy I sound. Maybe that book Linda bought me is working by osmosis or something. 'You brought it up, and if you refuse to clue me in... I'll... I'll... hold your dog hostage!'

Steve shoots a smile in my direction, and I find myself smiling right back... even though it's the last thing I want to do.

Stupid, traitorous face!

'Okay, fine,' he says, sliding the new lock into place and working quickly to secure it.

'You said something about Colin?' I prompt.

'Yeah. Colin,' says Steve with a frown. 'Well, from what Iris has told me, he's the root of your problems.'

'Tell me about it!' I mutter. 'But like I said, he's got nothing to do with Billingham's!'

Even as I say it, images of those business cards flash in my mind's eye.

Colin Sloan – Managing Director.

Sloan's Finest Chocolates.

'You need to ask the Angels for the details,' says Steve. 'But the general gist I got from Aunty Iris is that Colin told everyone they'd be losing their jobs.'

'That's rubbish,' I say, shaking my head irritably. 'Besides, they all know me too well to listen to anything like that. I mean, I think most of them came to my flippin' christening!'

'Yes – but this is your *husband* we're talking about,' says Steve carefully.

'Ex-husband!' I snap indignantly. 'Or nearly, at least.'

'Well, exactly!' he says, as though he's just explained everything.

'I don't get it!' I say.

'Look, it's like this,' he says, clearly resigning himself to the fact that I'm going to keep badgering him until I've extracted the details. 'You guys were still together when Alf died, right?'

'Just about,' I nod.

'Right, and your Gramps left the company to you?'

I nod again, but I'm still not getting it.

'Then you split up and file for divorce?'

I cringe.

'And everyone knows that assets are divided up in a divorce,' he says. 'So suddenly, the Angels think you're going to have to sell Billingham's to give half of it to Colin.'

'But – why didn't they just ask me?!' I gasp.

'Because you were already going through more than enough as it was,' he says, looking surprised. 'They care about you Holly – and you'd just lost your Gramps and then your husband left too!'

I nod slowly but then stop. 'But wait – you said Colin *told* them something?'

'You got back together, didn't you?'

Okay – now would be a good time for the floor to open up and swallow me whole.

'It was a mistake,' I mutter. 'I was in a mess.'

'Hey – you don't need to explain anything to me,' he says quickly. 'But apparently, during that time, he visited Billingham's.'

I wrack my brain, trying to remember. Steve's right. During Colin's seriously short-lived charm offensive, he did come and surprise me at work to take me out on a date.

'Well – according to Aunty Iris, he told everyone that Billingham's was going to be "modernised and streamlined." He told everyone that he'd be taking over as Managing Director and that most of them would be losing their jobs.'

'He said that?' I gasp. No wonder there's been an atmosphere!

'Apparently so,' Steve shrugs.

'But we split up again about two weeks later!' I say. 'And that was ages ago – right back in the spring! Why didn't anyone come to me?'

'All I know is that it's got something to do with some graphic design company?' says Steve. 'They've been phoning for Colin and Iris said they're still working on a rebrand…'

I suddenly feel like I've been driven into by a herd of decidedly pissed-off reindeer. 'Curves,' I breathe.

'Pardon?'

'The design company!' I say. 'Something came through from them this morning! I was going to follow it up with Doris as soon as the Christmas rush is over. I can't believe this!' I pause and run my fingers through my hair. 'So... basically everyone's spent most of the year thinking their jobs are on the line?'

Steve nods slowly. 'And... I'm taking it they're not?'

'Are you kidding me?' I laugh. 'Iris and Doris and all the others are the heart of that place. There's no rebranding. No modernisation. No lay-offs and *definitely* no Colin!'

'And...' he pauses for a second, 'sorry - this is a bit tricky...'

'Spit it out, Steve,' I sigh. 'We've gone way past tricky here! I want to put things right... and the only way I'm going to manage that is to know exactly what's going on!'

'Okay, fair point,' he says with a shrug. 'I was just going to say... you're still getting a divorce, right?'

'Hopefully in a matter of days!' I say with a growl.

'Oh. Good,' he says, then clears his throat. 'But... doesn't that still leave you with the problem of having to sell the business to split it with him?'

I gape at him as the last piece of the puzzle finally clicks into place. Of *course* that's what they all think. No wonder things have been so strained – the Angels have been waiting for me to tell them they're all out of a job.

'So… is it true?' he says. 'Are you going to have to sell?'

'Nope,' I say. 'Definitely not.'

'Seriously?' says Steve.

I nod. 'Gramps wasn't born yesterday. He never liked Colin much – and when he wrote his will, he made sure Billingham's would pass safely into my hands… and only my hands… whether I was wearing a wedding ring or not!'

'Thank heavens for Alf!' says Steve, blowing out a breath. 'And… just for the record… that makes me so happy. I can't wait to see what Aunty Iris says when she finds out. She's been so worried!'

I nod sadly. Nothing I say right now is going to make that any better, so I crouch down and wrap my arms around Arthur – Christmas jumper and all - and bury my face in his soft fur. I can hear his tail thumping on the carpet, and it's the only thing that stops me from bursting into tears.

'Yeah… he's good for that!' I hear Steve say quietly.

'Sorry…' I mumble into Arthur's neck. 'I promise I'll give your dog back in a sec.'

'No rush,' he says. 'Did you want me to take a look at your back door too while I'm here?'

The back door leads straight from the kitchen into my enclosed back garden. It's surrounded by a nice sturdy wooden fence… but I nod anyway.

'Please!' I mutter.

'Okay. You two hug it out,' he says. 'I'll be back.'

CHAPTER NINE

WE WISH YOU A GRUMPY CHRISTMAS, WE
WISH YOU A GROUCHY CHRISTMAS, WE
WISH YOU A STROPPY CHRISTMAS...

I'm nervous as I approach the familiar entrance to Billingham's, and not even the twinkling garland above the door can bring a smile to my face this morning. I'm so grateful to Steve for spilling the beans yesterday - but I have to admit that his bombshell about why the Angels have been more demonic than usual led to a pretty rough night's sleep.

I've got months of mistakes to put right... I just hope they'll all forgive me. Ah well... no time like the present! This morning's going to be awkward, to say the least - but the only way out of this mess is through.

First things first, though - I need a coffee. Then I need to thank Iris for putting me in touch with Steve in the first place. If this morning goes well, there's a good chance that man has sorted out more than just a new front door lock!

I clutch the potted Christmas rose I'm carrying

closer to my chest and force a smile onto my face. After all – it's good news I'm about to give everyone – in theory, at least. I just hope I don't dissolve into a pool of tears while I'm at it.

'Morning Holly!'

Doris scuttles up to me the moment I step through the doors and thrusts a steaming mug in my direction. I take a sniff hoping she hasn't mint-tea-d me again.

'It's coffee!' she says, lifting an eyebrow.

'Thanks,' I say, smiling at her.

Glory hallelujah - she smiles right back, and for the first time in forever, there seems to be some genuine warmth behind it. Something deep inside my chest relaxes a tiny bit, and I take an easy breath for the first time today.

'So,' she says, 'how did it go with the locksmith last night?'

'Spot on,' I say. In more ways than I care to admit right now - but Doris doesn't need to know the details yet. Not until I've had the chance to speak to Iris first. 'He was great,' I add when I catch her watching me closely. 'He sorted out the front door lock for me, and I think he's coming back to replace the one on the back door too.'

'That sounds like a very good idea,' she says blandly.

I nod. I suspect she'd quite like to launch into a Colin-related rant and is only holding off out of respect for me. Little does she know I plan to give all of them the chance to rant as much as they want very shortly!

'Lovely flowers,' she says, peaking at the potted rose.

'Thanks,' I say glancing down at the cheery-red blooms. 'I wanted to thank Iris properly - for trusting me with Steve's number.'

'Lovely thought,' says Doris approvingly. 'You know… we'd all do just about anything for you, Holly.'

The forthright way Doris says this while holding my eyes is ridiculously unnerving, and the lump of emotion that seems to have been hovering all morning rises into my throat and threatens to throttle me. I do my best to swallow it, but that just makes it overflow into my eyes instead.

'Thanks,' I eventually manage to choke out, blinking hard. 'I mean it.'

Doris nods.

I clear my throat again. This is getting silly.

'I need to catch Iris a moment before she launches into today's cards,'

'She's already at it!' says Doris. 'Last two days before the final post!'

'I know,' I say. 'We're nearly there - thanks to you.'

I'm not sure if it's the light, but I swear Doris just blushed!

'Thanks for holding the fort last night, by the way,' I say as she shifts uncomfortably. 'Was everything okay after I left?'

'All fine,' she says, clearly glad to be back onto practical topics. 'We all stayed an extra half an hour, so we're definitely going to be able to finish the orders with no problem.'

'You didn't have to do that!' I gasp, suddenly feeling guilty for leaving early.

'We enjoy it, Holly,' says Doris gently. 'That's the point - this is home for all of us... even more than our own houses for some of us, I suspect. Especially those of us who live alone.'

I nod as the reality of what she's saying hits me in the gut. Billingham's has always been special for me because of its connection to Gramps, but I have to admit I've never really considered that it might be the same for the others... that it's more than just their workplace.

Suddenly, everything Steve told me last night seemed to grab me by the throat.

'Everything okay?' says Doris, watching me closely.

'Honestly – I don't think it has been for a while now,' I say, 'but... I think I know why.'

'Oh?' says Doris going wide-eyed.

'Will you give me ten minutes with Iris, and then call everyone together? I think we need a staff meeting.'

Doris looks mildly panicked and I watch as a spike of fear crosses her face.

'It's all positive - I promise,' I say quickly. I don't want her to worry for a single second longer than she already has. 'It's just time for all of us to have a proper chat… it's been too long.'

Doris nods and takes a deep breath, visibly pulling herself together. 'I'll put the tea urn on too, shall I?'

'You've always been able to read my mind!' I say with a smile.

'Ever since you were a tiny thing, begging us to slip you chocolates!' she laughs.

'I've changed a bit since then,' I sigh.

'Actually, I don't think so,' she says, shaking her head. 'Not deep down where it counts. I've got a feeling you're still that little girl we've all loved for years.'

'Oh don't!' I say. My voice comes out in a decided wobble. 'I'm going to be an emotional wreck before I even start at this rate!'

'Fair enough,' she says. 'You go to Iris and I'll start rounding up the troops.'

'Ta,' I say.

'Erm… one thing though?' says Doris as I turn away.

'Mm?'

'Is it okay to tell everyone it's good news – like you said?' she says. I can't help but notice there's a pleading note in her voice. 'None of us is as young as we were… and I don't fancy giving anyone a heart attack just before Christmas.'

'Of course!' I say quickly. 'Good call. And I promise - it's true. This is all good, okay?'

'Iris!' I say as soon as she pops her pen down to blot the card she's been working on.

'Oh - hello!' she says, looking mildly surprised to find me standing here.

'Hi,' I say. 'This is for you.' I hold out the rose and after a beat, Iris reaches for it, her eyes wide behind her jewelled glasses.

'For me?' she says. 'It's... beautiful! Thank you... but... why?'

She looks so surprised by the gift that it makes my heart twist in my chest. I watch her take a delicate sniff of one of the little flowers, her smile broadening as she catches its sweet scent. These people are important. They're my family - and I've not been giving them enough of the care and attention they deserve.

'I wanted to say thank you for putting me in touch with Steve,' I say. 'He's already been brilliant.'

'He's a good lad!' says Iris proudly. 'And it's no trouble at all. I'm glad he could help!'

'Would you mind... if I borrow you for a moment?' I say, my nerves ramping up again. 'Can we have a chat in the office?'

'Oh no,' says Iris, suddenly looking like she's about to burst into tears. 'I've been dreading this.'

'It's not what you think - I promise!' I say quickly, shaking my head. 'It's good news.'

By the look on Iris's face, she doesn't believe a word

of it. Doris's words of warning about heart attacks ring in my ears.

'Pass me my stick, Holly?' says Iris. She's gone white, and I feel awful as I reach for her floral walking cane and hand it over to her.

'Take my arm,' I say, going to her side so that she can grab hold of my elbow as she struggles out of her chair. I can feel her quivering.

'Sorry!' she laughs. 'I'm all of a fluster!'

'It's fine,' I say gently. 'Take your time.'

'No other way!' says Iris.

We shuffle our way into Gramps's office and I help Iris make herself comfortable on the padded chair behind my desk.

'Sorry to take your seat, Holly, but I'd never get out of that settee!' she says, dangling her cane from the edge of my desk. 'I used to get stuck in it twenty years ago… goodness knows what would happen now. You'd probably need a winch to get me out of there!'

I grin at her.

'Right – you'd better put me out of my misery,' she sighs, her fingers clutching nervously at the edge of the desk. 'What's this all about?'

I plonk myself down onto a wooden stool and smile at her. 'Okay - Steve made me aware of a couple of things last night.'

'That boy's always been a blabbermouth,' she sighs.

I grin at her as she rolls her eyes.

'I've called a staff meeting in ten minutes,' I say.

'And it's all good news for everyone - okay?' I say again, hoping it might actually sink in this time.

'Okay,' says Iris, but I see her knuckles turn white as her fingers tighten on the edge of the desk.

'I just want to check things with you first,' I say, 'as it was Steve who told me…'

'Better to hear it from the horse's mouth?' says Iris.

'Exactly!' I nod. 'Plus, I don't want to make everything worse by mistake.'

'I don't think you can,' says Iris solemnly. 'Make everything worse, I mean. We've all been waiting for bad news from you for a good while now.'

'Mmm,' I say, feeling my hackles rise. It's not the Angels I'm angry with, it's Colin for causing this mess in the first place… and myself for not doing something about it sooner. 'So - here's the question. What do you all think is going to happen?'

'Well… we're kind of divided into two camps,' says Iris, suddenly looking embarrassed. 'Personally, I think you're going to be forced to sell Billingham's against your will because of your divorce. That's what most of us think. And then the factory will either be closed down, or the company will end up in someone else's hands entirely.'

'Right,' I say, shaking my head.

'And, of course, no one in their right mind is going to want a factory full of septuagenarians!'

'Clearly, I'm not in my right mind, then,' I say briskly.

'Goes for all the best people, dear,' says Iris with a rueful grin.

'True,' I say. 'So... what do the rest of them think?'

I'm not really sure I want to know this... but now that I've come this far, I might as well get the full picture.

'They think you're not going to go through with the divorce,' she says. 'They reckon you're going to take *him* back again, and then the place will become Sloane's instead.'

Iris pauses, and I suck in a deep breath.

'I think I know you better than that, though,' she continues. 'That man's gone for good this time - but it's hard to convince everyone when that graphic design company keeps calling Doris and asking to speak to Colin. Plus, *that* doesn't help!' Iris raises her hand and points across the office.

'What?' I say in surprise, turning my head. At first, I think she's pointing at one of the many Christmas cards lining the walls, but then I spot it...

'The photo,' she says.

I nod. It's in a wooden frame and is partially obscured by season's greetings – but I know exactly what it is. It's a photograph of me and Colin – back when we were just married and I thought we were happy. I gave it to Gramps as a birthday present years ago, and it must have sat on that shelf ever since. I can't say I've ever taken any notice of it - it's just part of the furniture... something that's practically invisible because it's always been there. It won't be there for much longer, that's for sure!

'Thank you for filling me in,' I say as soon as I'm sure I've got my voice under control.

'Please Holly - set my mind at rest before we go back out there?' says Iris. 'That lot will take ages pouring tea and settling down – and I'm not sure my poor old heart can handle the suspense!'

'Of course,' I say. 'Well – for one thing - you're right. Colin is gone for good. The divorce is nearly finalised.'

'Oh good,' says Iris, her eyes wide. 'And what about that design company he's been working with?'

'No rebrand,' I say. 'And definitely no new Managing Director! Billingham's is perfect just the way it is.'

'I agree,' says Iris. 'And… you're not going to lose it in the divorce?'

'No,' I say, letting out a huge sigh. 'I think Gramps knew what was coming. He made sure Billingham's is safe and sound and that I'm well looked after – despite my awful ex.'

Tears well in Iris's eyes and she whips out a fine lace handkerchief from her pocket. 'I'm sorry,' she says dabbing at her eyes. 'I've just been so worried.'

'Oh, Iris!' I say, reaching over and awkwardly patting her arm. 'I'm so sorry. I never wanted any of you to worry about your jobs! They'll be here as long as you want them. So will Billingham's!'

'I wasn't worried about that, you ninny!' Iris mumbles. 'I've been worried about you!'

I go still as a strange fizzing sparkle travels down my arms and spine.

'Me?' I say.

Iris nods. 'Losing Alf… taking over the reins here… and then that scoundrel doing what he did… twice!'

'Well, there's no need to worry about that anymore,' I say quickly. 'He's gone.'

'But we lost a little bit of you too there, for a while,' says Iris.

'I'm fine,' I say. 'I guess I've just been a bit sad.'

'That's the problem,' says Iris. 'That's why we've all been so worried. If you'd been angry or had a bit of fight in you, he'd never have been able to pull the wool over your eyes!'

I nod. Iris is right.

'You should go for someone like my Steve. Lovely boy. Single too! Colin never did deserve you,' she adds, throwing a dirty look at the framed photo.

'No,' I sigh, 'maybe not. But even worse - I'm not sure I deserve to have you and the rest of the Angels on my side.'

'Get on with you, girl!' says Iris, suddenly stern. 'For one thing – we're family, and deserving doesn't come into it. You don't need to earn your place – you already belong. For another thing - Alf would be proud of how you've kept things going at Billingham's this year.'

'That's nothing to do with me,' I say. 'That's you and Doris and the others.'

'Rubbish,' says Iris. 'Thanks to all your new-fangled videos and photos on the interwebs - we've had the best Christmas this company has ever seen.'

I raise my eyebrows.

'You just ask Doris yourself if you don't believe me,' says Iris with a smile. 'But first... I think it's time you put that lot out of their miseries too, don't you?'

I follow her gaze to the little window that looks out over the factory floor, and from my vantage point, I can see an entire thunderhead of grey hair waiting for us. The Angels have congregated right outside, and from what little I can see, it looks like they're very deliberately *not* looking through the window.

'Poor dears... they'll be right jealous you spoke to me first!' chuckles Iris.

'Let's do it then,' I say. 'But first - thank you!'

'I've already told you - it's no skin off my nose, sending Steve over to help you!'

I shake my head and smile. 'I don't mean just that. I mean... thank you for doing what you do. Billingham's wouldn't be the same without you.'

'I'm the one who needs to thank you for keeping me on,' she says. 'I know it would be cheaper and quicker to have a machine doing my job. In fact... Colin made sure to tell me exactly that.'

'Well... that goes to show the man has no taste, and

no clue what he's talking about!' I huff. 'Because our fans adore you. So… please stay!'

'Don't worry, dearie,' she laughs. 'I'm not going anywhere. Well… apart from out there because it looks like Doris has put the urn on and I know Gwen brought us all doughnuts!'

'Right then, lead the way!' I laugh, holding out my hand to help Iris back to her feet. Two seconds later, she's striding out of the office - leaving her floral cane still dangling from the edge of Gramps's desk.

CHAPTER TEN

THEY SAY PATIENCE IS A VIRTUE, BUT SO IS FINDING CREATIVE WAYS TO UNTANGLE CHRISTMAS LIGHTS WITHOUT LOSING THE PLOT

I look around at the waiting faces and instantly want to scuttle back to the office. But my days of burying my head in the sand are well and truly over… they have to be. Talking to Iris has just made me realise how close I've come to ruining what we have here.

Everyone's watching me nervously. A couple of the Angels have their arms crossed tightly and they look anything but happy. Doris is smiling, but she still looks decidedly uncomfortable. Iris is the only one who looks completely relaxed and happy as she tucks into a jam doughnut with gusto.

'Hi,' I say. 'It's been too long since I talked to you all properly.'

There are a couple of nods, and I let out a little sigh.

'Look,' I say. 'I know that there are loads of rumours floating around – and I want to make sure you all know exactly what's what. I'll answer any questions you can throw at me, but first I want you all to know that your jobs are safe. Also - nothing is changing. Billingham's isn't being sold, it's not being rebranded, and it's *definitely* not getting a new Managing Director in the shape of my idiot ex-husband!'

'So…' Edna glares at me from the back. She's one of our best packers and can do things with Christmas ribbon that I can't even begin to understand… 'so you're saying Colin hasn't got anything to do with the place anymore?'

'Anymore?' I say. 'He never has. Whatever he's said, whatever he's done… is lies… and basically not allowed. Yes - we are getting a divorce. Yes - he cheated on me. Twice.'

There's the sound of thunder as a dozen Angels grumble in horror at this admission.

'But,' I say loudly so that they can hear me over the rumbling, 'that's not important. What's important is that he doesn't even get a sniff at Billingham's. Thanks to Gramps - Alf - this place is ours.'

'Yours,' says Iris beaming.

'Mine,' I concede. 'But Billingham's was never about one person. It's about all of us. We're family.'

'Hear hear!' cheers Gwen.

'We're doing better than ever, and that's all down you lot!' I say.

There's an even louder rumble at this, and I see

several of the Angels giving Doris a prod. There are various mutterings of *tell her! Tell her!*

'Tell me what?' I say, suddenly off track as images of a mass walk-out pop into my head. I swallow hard - because without Alf's Angels on my side, Billingham's Finest Chocolates might as well close right now.

'It's not all down to us, dear,' says Doris.

The others nod.

'You… on those… thingies on the computer…' she continues, 'that's what's added so many new customers to our list. That's what's made this our best Christmas in years… probably ever!'

'Three cheers!' shouts someone from the back. I think it was Dawnie… but all I can see is a nibbled doughnut being waved enthusiastically.

There's a lot of giggling and nodding, and even a cheer or two.

'The point is, we're a team - and you're part of that,' says Doris. 'You always have been - ever since you were a little tacker.'

'And now you're a brilliant boss, and your Gramps would be proud!' says Edna.

Wasn't I meant to be the one giving the inspirational speech right now?

'Thanks, guys,' I say, my voice coming out thick and husky with emotion. 'You're seriously the best family I could ever wish for.'

'And on that note,' says Doris, 'sorry to break up the party, but the family need to get back to work if we're going to get all the orders ready in time for the last post. Twenty more came in this morning!'

There's a great deal of happy chattering as everyone makes their way back towards their various stations - but not one of them goes without giving me a squeeze on my arm or a pat on my back first.

'It's good to have you back, boss!' says Doris.

'Ta,' I say, smiling at her. 'I'm just… I'm just…' I point at the office.

Doris smiles at me and nods, understanding that I need a second to let it all sink in.

I let myself into the office and silence descends. All I can think right now is thank heavens for Steve. If he hadn't let the cat out of the bag last night, I might not have managed to untangle this mess before it was too late.

I take a deep breath, trying to calm down… but I don't think that's going to happen any time soon. I came so close to losing all this… all because of Colin. I can't quite figure out what he was trying to achieve - spreading lies amongst the Angels like that. Maybe it doesn't matter… maybe he just wanted to make my life as miserable as possible.

I turn on the spot and scan the shelves for the photograph of us together. It *has* to go. He doesn't belong at Billingham's in any way shape or form!

Grabbing the frame and sending several cards flying in the process, I stare at it. We're both smiling and Colin's arm is around me. We look so happy. It was taken during that brief spell before I realised I'd managed to get myself hitched to a mean-spirited git. I just wish it hadn't taken me so long to realise that I deserve so much more - and that my life could be a much happier place without him in it.

I stare at it for a long moment... and for the first time, I don't feel sad... I feel...

Hot...

Bothered...

Fidgety...

I let out a long, slow breath, trying to quell a wave of anger as it crashes over me. This man cheated on me. Twice. He tried to steal the company from me - the company my Gramps built. He tried to turn the Angels against me... and he tried to come over to the cottage the other night to talk everything through?

'I hate you!' I mutter at the photo in my hands, my fingers turning white as my grip tightens. He's never apologised. Sure, maybe I'm a little bit to blame for taking him back and giving him a second chance... but that's never happening again.

'Goodbye!' I hiss at the photo, and then with a flick of my wrist, I toss it directly into the waste paper basket.

If I'm honest - it's a massive anti-climax. There's no tinkle of shattering glass or crack of splintering wood. It just lands with a kind of deadened thump and sits there staring up at me.

'You can do better than that!' comes a voice from

behind me. I glance over my shoulder only to find Doris watching me.

'You weren't supposed to see that!' I mutter as my cheeks begin to flush. Jeez… the one and only time I try to let kind of anger bubble up and I do a half-arsed job of it. Not only that - I manage to get caught in the act too!

Doris strides over to the bin and retrieves the intact frame. I hang my head. I swear, if she puts it back on the shelf, I'm going to dissolve into a heap of shame.

Instead, she comes to stand next to me and hands the blasted thing back to me.

'Tell him what you think of him,' she says.

'It's okay,' I say. 'I don't-'

'Tell him!' demands Doris.

'I hate him?' I say, looking at her.

'Don't ask me, girl!' she laughs. 'Tell him.'

'Colin, I hate you,' I say to the frame.

'Now say it like you mean it!'

'I hate you!' I say, surprised to hear a growl creep into my tone.

'Now tell him why,' she prompts

'I don't…'

'Tell him!' says Doris, her voice ringing out and bouncing around the office.

'You cheated on me,' I say.

I pause and wait for Doris's next command, but she just stands quietly by my side. I can feel her solid presence backing me up - and suddenly I feel like I have permission to really let rip.

'I hate you for making me feel small. I hate you for making me miss so much time with my Gramps,' my words are starting to trip over themselves now, but I'm not done yet. 'I hate you for making me doubt myself. I hate you for trying to turn my family against me. I hate you for every tear I've ever cried because of you. I hate you for every Christmas I've missed. I hate you for not loving me like I deserve to be loved!'

I pause, my breathing is ragged and I want to reach into the frame and wring his scrawny little neck.

'Anything else you want to say to him before we dispose of him for good?' says Doris.

I shake my head, unable to stop a smile from creeping onto my face. I wonder if she realises she's just crossed the line from consoling confidant to scary mobster.

'Throw it, then!' she says.

I take a step towards the bin.

'Don't wimp out on me, Billingham!' she says. 'Straight down. Onto the floor!'

I glance at her and raise an eyebrow. 'Won't that make a mess?'

Doris rolls her eyes. 'Did he or did he not make a mess of your life?'

I nod, resisting the urge to grind my teeth.

'Did he or did he not break your heart?' she all but shouts.

I nod again.

'Then throw it!'

'I-'

'THROW IT!'

I raise the frame high in the air and hurl it at the concrete floor.

The crashing, splintering sound is the final full stop I've been craving. There it is - the end to him and all his nonsense. Divorce papers or no - my *almost*-ex-husband has just crossed the line into completely and most definitely done with EX.

I reach out blindly and Doris takes my hand, giving my fingers a solid squeeze.

'You're scarily good at that, you know!' I laugh as a tear of pure relief escapes and trickles down my cheek.

'I know!' she says, squeezing my hand again. 'Right… I'll go and get the dustpan and brush, shall I?'

'One sec,' I say.

I take a step towards the mess and, aiming right for Colin's face, I grind the heel of my boot into glass, wood and photograph.

'There. That's better,' I say. 'Don't worry - I'll grab the brush and tidy this lot up!'

Doris shakes her head. 'First - you've got a call waiting for you on line two.'

'Waiting for me?' I gasp, staring at the mess on the floor again and then back to Doris. 'All this time?'

'You were in the middle of something important!' she says with a shrug.

'But…' I'm about to argue, but then I realise I don't want to. Doris is right. 'Who is it?' I say instead.

'That graphic design company,' she smirks. 'The one Colin hired? And… I'd say we've just got you into the perfect frame of mind to deal with them!'

CHAPTER ELEVEN

ANGER MANAGEMENT TIP: IF YOU FIND
YOURSELF ABOUT TO EXPLODE – GRAB A
CHRISTMAS CRACKER AND SHOUT "BANG!"

*B*y the time I get back to the cottage, I'm practically dragging my feet with tiredness. Today has been weirdly emotional, completely full on… and one of the best days I've had in ages.

There was a lot of laughter as we all worked our behinds off to get our new orders packed. Stocks are running low for some of our favourite Belgian delicacies… but there's just about enough left to finish our Christmas season at Billingham's with a flourish.

I smile as I mooch towards my cottage. I can't wait to take my boots off and pour myself a bath. I'm thinking a hot chocolate slurped while enjoying plenty of bubbles is needed before I even consider doing anything else. After that… I'm going to open my new tartan Christmas PJs early.

What a rebel!

I grin at the thought… only for the smile to fade on

my face when I spot the garden gate. It's open and swinging on its hinges. I cross my fingers it's just because I've had a delivery while I've been at work… but I can't see any sign of a package, and the delivery guy is usually very good at closing it behind him.

Then, I spot Eileen's net curtain flickering next door and brace myself. My lovely next-door neighbour is a force to be reckoned with. She's very forthright, but about as kind a neighbour as I could wish for.

'Holly!' she calls, her smiling face appearing at her front door. 'Good- I was hoping to catch you. You're late home - got a new fancy man?'

I grin at her. Coming from anyone else, this might feel a bit barbed, but Eileen's been asking me the same question since I first met her - even when I was still living with Colin!

'Fraid not,' I heave a dramatic sigh. 'Just working late to get the Christmas orders packed before the cut-off!'

'Oh, shame,' she says with a chuckle as she scuttles along her front path towards me. 'I was hoping that bit of stuff I saw you with last night might be on the scene!'

I swear I can't get a single thing past Eileen! I'm sure she wishes I was a bit more interesting so that she had something more interesting than my weekly grocery delivery to spy on!

'I'm afraid that was just Steve the locksmith!' I

chuckle. 'And his dog Arthur - who I *might* have fallen a little bit in love with!'

'Well... that does explain things,' she says tapping her chin thoughtfully.

'Things?' I say. 'What things?'

'Well... it's like this,' she says, puffing out her chest like she always does when she's got a good bit of gossip to impart. 'I caught that Colin of yours trying to climb over my back fence earlier.'

'Wait... what?!' I say.

'Colin. He was trying to get into your garden,' she says more slowly.

'What time?!' I say as I try to process this nugget of particularly horrible information.

'Midday,' says Eileen. 'I know because I was just waiting for the news to come on the radio. Basically... when you were pretty much guaranteed to be at work!'

I scrunch my nose up. I'd been hoping that I wouldn't have to think about him again today after my photo-smashing routine with Doris earlier.

'Don't worry,' she says, 'he didn't make a very good job of it at all. He had a large suitcase on wheels with him... that made getting over the fence pretty much impossible!'

'A suitcase?' I gasp.

'A heavy one,' she nods.

Well, I guess at least it wasn't an empty one... that would have been even more worrying.

'He was trampling all over the patch I've planted my

spring bulbs - so I went out and gave him an earful!' she says gleefully.

'What did he say?' I ask. I'm not sure I even want to know, if I'm honest... but forewarned is forearmed. Plus – it doesn't sound like he got the chance to get inside the cottage thanks to Eileen, so no doubt that he'll be back.

'Oh, he blathered on about not being able to get through the front door,' she says. 'Kept saying the lock must be broken.'

'Right,' I say.

'Then he asked me if I had a spare, or if I knew where you hid one.'

'He did?!' I say.

'Cheeky blighter!' Eileen nods. 'I wasn't going to tell him I keep one for you in the hallway drawer, was I?'

'Thank you,' I say. 'It wouldn't have helped him if you'd given it to him anyway - I got the lock changed yesterday.'

'Hm,' says Eileen. 'He kept telling me that you were on your way and you knew he was going to be there.'

'No, and no,' I say with a little shiver.

'Don't you worry, Holly my love,' says Eileen kindly. 'I didn't get to sixty-seven years old without the ability to see straight through that man.

I grin at her. I know for a fact that Eileen is in her mid-eighties because her date of birth was printed on the prescription I picked up for her a couple of weeks ago. Her secret is safe with me though!

'How did you get rid of him in the end?' I ask. Colin's hard to shake when he's up to something.

'Well, I told him to sling his hook, didn't I!' says Eileen 'He was trespassing in my garden. When you speak to him, tell him if there's any sign of damage to my fence when I've had a proper look - and if my bulbs don't come up in the spring - he's going to have to cough up for repairs and replacements!'

'I will,' I chuckle. 'Though with any luck, I won't have to speak to him again. I've had enough of him.'

'Well… I'm not sure you're going to get away with that I'm afraid,' says Eileen. 'Something tells me he'll be back.'

I fidget at the thought as she watches me in concern.

'Thanks for keeping an eye on my place for me,' I say. 'I really appreciate it. I don't suppose you'd give me a quick call at Billingham's if you spot him snooping around again?'

'I certainly will!' says Eileen stoutly. 'I have to say, I rather enjoyed having a good shout at him. I never really liked him much and I'm glad you got rid of him.'

'I think it was more the other way around,' I sigh. 'He got rid of me. But thanks!'

Eileen shakes her head. 'No – you mark my words, it's *you* binning *him*, young lady. He might have started the ball rolling - but now it's up to you not to let him come crawling back.'

'No fear of that,' I say. 'Not this time.'

'Well, good,' says Eileen. 'Because he made a mess of my grass with the wheels of that case, you know!'

'I'm sorry, Eileen.'

'It's not something for you to apologise for!' she says. 'I'll just call the police next time,' she adds, looking thrilled at the idea.

'Actually - that would be great!' I say. 'I've got Steve coming back to fit the new back door lock for me tomorrow... but if he makes it over your fence before then, he'll be able to get in.'

'Don't you worry about that,' says Eileen, drawing herself up to her full height - all four feet eleven inches. 'I'll be on the lookout.'

'Thanks, Eileen,' I say. 'You're a good friend.'

The words have a peculiar effect. Eileen seems to soften around the edges as she turns all rosy and pink.

'Ah, you're a good girl,' she says, patting my cheek. 'And I'm very glad to hear that young man's coming back tomorrow. Him and his dog... both of them had kind faces.'

I nod and smile. 'They did.'

CHAPTER TWELVE

ANGER MANAGEMENT TIP: IF YOU CAN'T BEAT 'EM, AT LEAST TRY ANNOYING THEM UNTIL THEY GIVE UP

J'm just closing the door of the cottage behind me when the landline starts to ring. My heart promptly sinks right into my boots. I'm freezing from standing around talking to Eileen for too long, and I'm desperate for that bath and hot chocolate. I mean… I have serious plans to do some damage to a mound of squirty cream and mini marshmallows. I might even add a splash of Bailey's in there for good measure.

I sigh as I dash through to the living room and my X-rated hot-chocolate dream starts to fade. I've got a horrible feeling I know exactly who this is going to be… and it's the last person on earth I want to talk to right now. It's like I've somehow managed to summon the Grinch of Christmas Past just by talking about him too much today.

My hand hovers over the receiver. I *could* just

ignore it, couldn't I? But then - if I'm right and it *is* Colin, I *really* don't want him turning up at the cottage again. Of course… there's a slim chance it could be someone else less obnoxious…

Yeah right! I know how Colin operates - and this is almost guaranteed to be him. He'll be calling the landline instead of my mobile because he knows if I see his name flashing up on the screen, there's a good chance I'll just ignore it. Sadly, as cool as my ancient rotary phone is, it doesn't have anything as handy as caller ID!

Right… well… time to revert to type and answer the bloody thing, I guess!

'Holly Billingham!' I say, injecting as much cheerfulness into my voice as humanly possible - just to upset him.

'What's got into you?' he grumbles.

Point one to me!

I roll my eyes but then I grin to myself. I don't need to let him drag me down, do I? His perma-grouchiness has nothing to do with me anymore.

'I'm sorry… who is this?' I say lightly, the smile still in my voice.

'Oh for fu-'

'Sorry, I'm not buying anything today!' I say merrily, and replace the receiver, letting out a ridiculous giggle the minute it lands in its cradle.

That felt *so* good! I know, I know… I shouldn't be playing games - but that was stupidly satisfying.

I start counting and only get to three before the

phone rings again.

'Holly, it's Colin.'

'Colin? Hi!' I say cheerfully. 'You're lucky to reach me - I just got the *weirdest* phone call!'

'That was me!' he growls.

'It was?' I fake gasp. 'Why didn't you say so?'

'Whatever,' he huffs, and I have to quickly cover the mouthpiece to hide my snort of amusement. 'Your bloody neighbour needs putting into an old peoples' home,' he adds.

That makes me bristle, and the smile slides from my face. See, this is the problem - the man is just a solid-gold bottom-dweller.

'You still there?' he grumbles.

'Yes,' I say. *Unfortunately,* I add inside my own head.

'Don't say "yes" like that,' he starts.

'What do you want?' I sigh. 'I'm busy.'

'I want you to tell your bloody neighbour to be nicer to me next time I come over,' he says. 'I *am* your husband and-'

'No Colin, you're not,' I say, interrupting him. 'Plus - I believe she found you standing in *her* flower bed - in *her* garden - trying to climb *her* fence. Why should she be nice to you?!'

'Don't be like that, Holly Berry – I only came over to talk!' he says, his voice going all soft and whiney. Seriously, the man can change tack so fast that it gives me whiplash. 'You know I hate doing everything over the phone,' he wheedles. 'If we could just have a conversation face-to-face, I'm sure we could sort everything out.'

I shake my head in horror. I know he can't see me, but it's an automatic reaction.

'No chance, Colin,' I say. 'I mean - it didn't exactly help during all those years we were married, did it? I don't see why it should work now, do you?'

'I-'

'Besides,' I continue, not pausing long enough to let him start up again, 'I don't see what dragging a huge suitcase over here has anything to do with wanting a face-to-face conversation with me. Eileen said it was so heavy, you couldn't lift it over the fence!'

I pause. I'm intrigued to see what he's got to say for himself and his enormous case. All I get for a moment is heavy breathing - so I guess that answers that. Just as I'm starting to wonder if he's hung up on me he mumbles "Christmas Present?"

It's definitely more of a question than a statement.

'Uh huh?' I say, raising my eyebrows.

'What I want to know,' he says, rallying and changing direction again, 'is why my key doesn't work.'

'What I want to know,' I quickly counter, 'is why you still have a key to my cottage in the first place. It's one of the conditions of our divorce - in case you've forgotten. You're meant to have handed over your keys weeks ago.'

'It's still my house,' he mutters.

'No Colin, it's not,' I sigh. 'In fact - it's *never* been

your house.'

It's true. The cottage officially belonged to Gramps. He bought it as a rental property – and then asked us if we'd like to move in when we got married.

'When we lost him - when *I* lost him - he left it to me,' I say quietly.

'Yes - and we were married at the time,' says Colin, his voice rising in anger. 'In fact, we are still legally married. And that's why I get half.'

I pinch the bridge of my nose for a moment, wondering why I pay my divorce lawyer so much. Colin clearly doesn't read - or doesn't understand - anything the man sends to him!

'Why doesn't the key work, Holly?' Colin's voice now holds an edge I really don't like, and I shiver. I'm so glad I didn't come home to find him here. I make a mental note to buy something outrageously luxurious for Eileen for Christmas.

'Because you cheated on me,' I say. All pretence of warmth in my voice has well and truly gone now. 'Then, when I took you back - you cheated on me again - with the same woman.

'But if you remember-' he starts

I'm not in the mood to listen to how it was all my fault. Not this time - so I cut right across him.

'Because you tried to steal my business from me. Because you tried to turn the Angels against me. And because this is no longer your home. That's why the key doesn't work.'

'What… so it's like some sort of revenge magic?' he says.

'No, you dumbass,' I hiss. 'It's like some sort of lock-smith magic.'

'I cannot believe you'd do something like this,' he whines again, 'at Christmas too.'

'You don't celebrate Christmas,' I remind him. 'You're like one big sackful of anti-Christmas.'

'So - when are you going to give me the new spare key?' he says.

I can't help it, I stand for several long seconds and just gape down at the phone. If someone drew a cartoon of me right now, I'd have giant question marks hovering over my head.

'You don't get a spare,' I say slowly, feeling like I'm explaining this to a lump of solid rock. Actually, I think I'd probably have more luck getting the rock to understand! 'We are no longer together. In a few short weeks, we won't be married either. There's no reason for you to have a key. This is my house. This is my home. You. Do. Not. Live. Here.'

There - I don't think there's any way I could have said it plainer.

'I really think I should have one though - just in case of emergencies,' he says. 'What if someone tries to break in?'

I suddenly feel like I need to headbutt a wall.

Instead - I do the next best thing.

I hang up.

CHAPTER THIRTEEN

THEY SAY LAUGHTER IS THE BEST GIFT, BUT HAVE YOU TRIED WRAPPING YOUR ANGER IN TINSEL?

*W*e're all gathered around Edna's desk, watching as she ties the most intricate green and red bow I've ever seen.

'Three…' bellows Doris.

'Don't rush me!' grumbles Edna.

'Two!' shouts Gwen.

'Oi… what did I just say!'

'One!' I yell.

'And I'm finished!' cheers Edna, with a fist pump that would be more in keeping with a twenty-something footballer than an octogenarian who just tied the final bow of the Christmas season here at Billingham's.

Doris grabs the handbell and gives it a hearty shake, and the rest of us break into a round of rather rowdy cheers. Gwen shoves two fingers into her mouth and gives a series of piercing, celebratory whistles.

Suddenly, I'm giggling so hard I can feel tears

starting to form… though that might be from sheer relief. Our last Christmas order is wrapped and ready. We did it - we made our deadline! The postie is due for pick up in about half an hour and then the mad dash is officially over.

'You lot are incredible!' I say as the din calms down a bit, and I beam around at the Angels who're all looking decidedly pleased with themselves. It's just as well, because I'm still holding up my phone, and we've just live-streamed the whole thing. Now my mobile's busy vibrating like a trapped bee as likes and comments flood in from our fans all over the world. With any luck, there'll be a nice bundle of orders for New Year's treats pinging in too!

We don't need to worry about that right now, though. Christmas at Billingham's is a wrap – and all we've got left to do today is hand over the final parcels to the postie and then make a start on tidying up the factory ready for our brief Christmas break. The hard work is done, and the next few days will be spent eating mince pies, guzzling too much tea and warbling Christmas carols as we clean.

The bit I'm not looking forward to is saying good-bye. These last few days have been truly magical – and I'll be sad not to see the Angels over Christmas. I'll be celebrating the big day on my own… but at least this year I'll have a big smile on my face the entire time!

'It's official,' says Doris. 'This has been our best

Christmas season ever… and we've completely run out of Reindeer Poop.'

The Angels all start to snigger, and I can't help but join in. The glitter-encrusted, dark Belgian chocolates have been the biggest hit of the season - and that makes me so happy. It was the last new product Gramps chose for us before he passed away.

'We saved the last handful for Linda,' says Gwen, handing me a little, glittery pouch. 'Add it to her hamper!'

'I will,' I say, grinning at them. 'Thank you!'

'Why don't you leave us lot to it and head over to see her now?' says Doris.

'But-' I say. There's no way I want to skive off early and leave everyone else with the tidying up.

'It's fine!' laughs Doris. 'Your friend needs you - and if you're not here, it means the rest of us can skive off early too!'

She winks at me and I let out a surprised laugh.

'Okay- that's a deal,' I say. 'As soon as the postie has been - head home - all of you. You all deserve to put your feet up - we'll get on with the tidy-up tomorrow.'

'Don't mind if we do!' calls Edna, biting into one of the mince pies Gwen brought in to keep everyone's energy up today.

I take the Reindeer Poop into my office and head over to the big box I've been putting together for Linda. She needs something to cheer her up, poor thing! Last time I spoke to her, she was on her sofa wrapped in a duvet. She's come down with the office lurgy… something she's blaming on all the snogging she did with Danny from accounts at the Christmas party. It sounds like the mistletoe headband was something of a winner – even if the result wasn't quite what she'd been hoping for!

I flip open the lid of the huge Billingham's hamper and nestle the Reindeer Poop into the nest of tissue paper inside. It's already heaving with the best of the best - a full and delicious selection of everything we have to offer. After all… what's the point of owning a chocolate factory if I can't make the most of it to cheer up my best mate when she needs it?

I consider begging Edna to come and help me with the ribbons but then decide to give it a go myself. Iris has already let me borrow her gold ink to daub my very own card… and very kindly didn't make a comment on my less-than-elegant mess of a message. She did offer me calligraphy lessons in the new year, though!

I give the ribbon one last tweak and then heft the hamper into my arms and head out onto the factory floor.

'Let me look,' says Edna, appearing in front of me. I've got a sneaking suspicion she's been lying in wait right outside the office door. I angle the hamper towards her so that she can check out my masterpiece.

'Not bad,' she says with an approving nod. 'We'll make an Angel out of you yet!'

Hot tears instantly fill my eyes… and I grin at her with wobbling lips.

'You daft girl!' she chuckles, giving me a gentle pat on the arm. 'Alf would be proud of you, you know? But then… he always was.'

———

I hammer on Linda's front door with the toe of my boot and then take a step back, clutching her giant hamper under one arm. A bagful of cold and flu relief dangles from my other hand. On the way over here, I decided that - considering she probably won't be able to taste the chocolate at the moment - a bunch of vitamins, vapour rub and tissues might actually come in more handy.

I wait for several long seconds before there's some shuffling, and then the door finally opens. A grey-tinged Linda, wearing a ginormous fluffy hoodie and stripey socks, blinks at me blearily.

'Blimey girl,' I gasp. 'You look…'

'Gorgeous?' croaks Linda.

'Grey?' I counter.

'Bloody Danny,' she mutters. 'Come in.'

I wrinkle my nose. I'm not sure I want to enter the house of plague.

'Don't look at me like that!' she grumbles. 'As long as you're not planning on snogging me, I think you'll probably be okay!'

'I'll just keep my distance and gargle with some brandy later!' I grin as I follow her inside.

She leads me through to her cosy living room, and I have to hand it to her - she's doing the lurgy in style. There's a huge cashmere blanket draped over the sofa, evidence of a fancy ready meal on the coffee table, and an iPad paused mid-romcom.

'You looking after yourself?' I say sympathetically as she starts to cough.

'You'd better believe it!' she rasps. 'If I'm going down with the plague at Christmas, I'm going to do it in comfort.'

'Fair enough,' I say. 'Here - for when you can actually taste things again.' I hand over the massive Billingham's hamper and Linda's eyes go wide.

'Ooh yum!' she says. She might be grey and washed out right now, but chocolate always puts a smile on my best friend's face. 'If I wasn't quite so gross right now, I'd hug you.'

'Please don't!' I laugh. 'Besides, too much hugging at your Christmas party was what got you in this state in the first place.'

'Bit more than hugging!' she says before starting to cough again.

'You hussy!' I gasp.

'Yeah well... I blame the mistletoe headband!' she says, flopping down onto her sofa and drawing the blanket up to her chin. 'Worked like a charm!'

I sink into her posh, patchwork armchair – as far away from the patient as I can get.

'So,' I say. 'The question is, was Danny worth the wait… and the lurgy?'

'That's a no and no!' says Linda with a dramatic sigh.

'Oh no- really?'

She nods. 'Sloppy kisser.'

'Eww!' I say.

'You've got no idea,' she says, wrinkling her nose. 'Take sloppy and times it by about two hundred. I basically needed a towel afterwards.'

'Gross!' I squeak.

'You don't need to tell me that!' she laughs. 'Anyway – after that, I'm going to need to find a new job!'

I roll my eyes. My best friend - the drama queen!

'I'm serious,' she croaks, closing her eyes and leaning back. 'I had to drown the kiss with as much cheap wine and vol-au-vents as I could manage. It wasn't a good look.'

'Ah well,' I say. 'If you fancy swapping office management for chocolate, I've got a feeling we might be looking for some new Angels in the new year if things at Billingham's carry on at this pace!'

Linda smiles. 'That sounds more positive than last time I saw you.'

I nod. I've already filled her in on everything that's happened at the factory over the last few days.

'Yeah,' I say with a huge smile. 'Thank heavens for Steve being a blabbermouth!'

'Oh good,' says Linda, suddenly looking smug.

'What?' I say.

'You brought him up, so I don't have to!'

'You know,' I say, jumping to my feet, 'I think I'm going to head off and let you get some rest.'

Frankly – she's looking a lot better than she did just a couple of seconds ago... something to do with the fact she's gearing up to give me the third-degree about Steve, no doubt!

'Oh – I forgot – I got you this!' I say, handing over the pink carrier bag from the pharmacy. 'Goodies to get you better... because you're not going to be able to taste the chocolate in your condition!'

'You're a hero,' she says, peeping inside the bag and grabbing the box of Lemsip. 'But you're not getting away from me that easily!'

'I'm not?' I say.

'No way,' she laughs, shaking her head and then putting her hand to her forehead. Clearly, the move-ment was too much for her poor sinuses to handle. 'First - you're going to be a good girl and boil the kettle and make me one of these.' She tosses the box of Lemsip at me.

'Fair enough!' I laugh. Frankly, I don't mind Linda ordering me around. She's basically been my mother hen all year – clucking around me and looking after me as I tried to figure out which way was up. It's time to return the favour.

'Second,' she calls after me as I make my way through to the kitchen, 'you're going to come back and tell me *all* the juicy gossip about this locksmith of yours!'

'He's not *mine!*' I say firmly, popping open the old-fashioned serving hatch so that I can talk to her while the kettle boils.

'But… he's coming back?' she says.

'Yes. Tomorrow. He's going to Colin-proof the back door for me,' I say, giving a little shudder.

'What's he like?' she demands. 'I need visuals… I need to imagine exactly how this is going to go.'

'Go?' I say.

'He's going to sweep you off your feet for Christmas,' she says as if it's something she's ordered for me online.

'Bog off!' I laugh. 'You've clearly got a fever and are delirious.'

'Nope,' says Linda.

'In that case - it's too many romcoms!' I laugh, pouring boiling water over her flu powder, grabbing myself a cup of tea while I'm at it and heading back into the living room.

'Okay - there may have been a great deal of Hugh Grant action today,' she concedes, 'but there was some-thing about the way you said his name on the phone.'

She pauses to blow her nose. 'Steeeeeeeeve!' she croons at me as soon as she's done.

'You sure you're not high on cough medicine?' I chuckle.

'Come on, Hols,' she wheedles. 'I feel rubbish... let me live vicariously. What does he look like? Tell me anything!!'

I sip my tea, thinking hard. 'He's got nice hair,' I say at last, remembering the shiny caramel strands I instantly wanted to run my fingers through. 'And he's got a dog called Arthur who I think I'm a bit in love with.'

'That's all you've got for me?' she says, rolling her eyes. 'Hair and a dog?'

I shrug. It's all I'm giving her right now. I don't need Linda getting all excited about the weird fluttering feeling I had going on in my stomach the entire time Steve was at the cottage. Besides - as soon as he dropped the bombshell about the fact that Colin was busy trying to wreck my life some more – I kind of forgot about everything else!

'Sorry,' I say. 'I had other things on my mind.'

'Well... fine,' says Linda, sipping her drink. 'But that means I'm giving you homework!'

CHAPTER FOURTEEN

ANGER IS JUST A SNOWBALL FIGHT
WAITING TO HAPPEN

*a*s soon as I hear Steve's gentle knock on the front door, my stomach does a funny little backflip. Frankly, I blame Linda for putting ideas in my head.

Still - I've promised my best friend I'll pay more attention this time and find out more about him. Of course, I didn't tell her that it'll be absolutely no skin off my nose. I wouldn't admit it to anyone, but I can't wait to see him again.

Taking a deep, steadying breath, I throw open the front door.

'Hi!' I say

'Hey Holly!'

He's wearing that ridiculous bobble hat again – but that's not what's got me glued to the spot. It's that smile of his – it's been haunting me for days and now it's right in front of me.

'You okay?' laughs Steve.

I nod like an idiot and feel my face flush. It's no wonder he's looking at me a bit funny - I'm basically just standing here on the doorstep, gawping at him.

'Sorry, yeah!' I laugh. 'Come on in!'

'Is it okay if Arthur-'

Arthur, however, isn't up for waiting for his dad to ask the question. He must have been standing right behind Steve because the old dog barges past Steve's knees into the warmth of the hallway.

I grin and Steve shakes his head. 'Seriously, dude - where are your manners?!

'Old age perk, I think!' I chuckle, admiring today's jumper – which basically makes him look like a giant Christmas pudding.

'You might be right!' says Steve. 'Sorry Holly!'

'It's fine,' I say.

More than fine, actually. I've been hoping to see Arthur again – and this time, I'm prepared. I've heaped an old duvet on the kitchen floor in front of the radiator so that Arthur will be nice and warm and comfy while Steve works on the back door. There's a fresh pack of Rich Teas in there for him too.

'Come on through,' I say.

The three of us pile into the kitchen, and Arthur instantly spots the duvet and makes a beeline for it.

'Oh nooo!' gasps Steve as Arthur hops straight onto his makeshift bed and starts to make a nest.

'It' fine!' I laugh. 'I put it there for him!'

'You did?' says Steve, turning to me with such a full-wattage smile it takes my breath away.

I nod and try to force myself to breathe. It doesn't help. I get a waft of something lemony and woody. That's when I realise he's taken his hat off and his hair is damp... has the man just climbed out of the shower or something? It's the middle of the afternoon!

'Thanks,' he says.

I stare at him, completely confused.

'For Arthur's bed!' he says. 'And excuse the wet hair - I had to grab a shower before coming over.'

'Oh?' I say. Clearly the man really is a mind reader. I'm not sure how I feel about that right now considering my thoughts have just taken a turn for the X-rated. I blame the scent of woodsmoke and citrus! It's doing something strange to me.

'One of Iris's neighbours had a bit of an emergency,' he says, running self-conscious fingers through his damp hair and looking like something straight out of a shampoo advert. 'She had a blocked drain and I spent an hour clearing it out. Not exactly what I had planned - but hey, an emergency is an emergency, right?! And there was no way I was coming over here smelling of drains!'

I grin at him. I mean, I'm definitely not complaining. I make a mental note to add "smells nice and looks after old ladies" to my list of details for Linda.

'Can I give Arthur a biscuit?' I say, gesturing at a pack of Rich Teas on the counter. I need to get away from this fruity-smelling man for a second – for his own safety!

'Only if you want a best friend for life!' says Steve, plonking his toolbox down next to the counter and kneeling down to open it.

'And you?' I say, snapping a biscuit in half for Arthur.

'No thanks to the biscuit!' he says, smiling up at me.

My knees instantly start to bobble. What is it about handsome men down on one knee?

'I'm afraid I'm a spoiled brat when it comes to biscuits - Iris makes the most amazing homemade ones – she's ruined anything that comes out of a packet for me!' He shoots me a grin. 'I'd go for a cuppa, though - if there's one on offer? I didn't get a chance before heading over to you with all the drain action… I'm parched.'

'Of course!' I say, flicking the kettle on and then heading for Arthur's bed. He's already sitting up, his tail beating against the duvet as he eyeballs the treat in my hand. 'Here you go, gorgeous boy!' I croon.

I peep across at Steve only to find him chuckling as he watches me.

'What?' I demand.

'Nothing.' He shrugs.

Arthur, who's just wolfed down both halves of the biscuit in a matter of seconds, is now snuffling into my empty hands in case some more might magically appear.

'Let me get you a bowl of water,' I say. 'Milk in your tea, Steve?'

'Milk - no sugar, ta!' he says.

I busy myself getting the boys their drinks but when I turn to hand a mug to Steve, I find him staring at the back door with a scowl on his face.

'What's up?' I say in surprise.

'What's this about?' he says, gesturing towards the wooden chair I've got rammed up against the door, wedged firmly under the handle.

'Oh... erm... nothing?' I try.

'Holly?' he rumbles.

'Okay - fine. It's my very high-tech anti-almost-ex-husband device!' I laugh, doing my best to break the weird tension that has just descended on the room.

'I see,' he says. 'Iris told me a bit about him... she said he was a bit of a problem.'

'Uh huh?' I say.

'She didn't say it was *this* kind of problem, though.'

He's practically growling now, and as much as I appreciate the protective vibes that are practically rippling off him, I do feel like I need to put him straight... just in case he ever bumps into Colin. Judging by the look on Steve's face right now - I've got a feeling my ex might be in some serious physical danger otherwise.

'It's not like that,' I say, going to lay a hand on his arm and then thinking better of it.

'Like what?' says Steve.

'You know... he's never been... like that?' I say. 'Physical.'

'Let me ask you a question?' he says.

'O-kay?' I say, even though I'd really prefer it if we rewound things by about sixty seconds and went back to the nice, calm, slightly flirty cuppa in the kitchen we were about to enjoy.

'Has he tried to break in here?' says Steve.

'No... yes... no...' I answer, clearing things up beautifully.

'Let's go with the *yes* part of that answer, shall we?' says Steve. 'What happened.'

I let out a long sigh and shoot daggers at the chair for telling tales on me.

'Fine,' I sigh. 'It's not a huge deal because my elderly neighbour caught him.'

'Caught him doing what?!' demands Steve. The man's vibrating with frustration and I see him flex one large, surprisingly strong-looking hand.

I swallow. 'He tried to let himself into the cottage a couple of days ago,' I say. 'I was at work. When his key didn't work - he thought he'd have a go at the back door instead.'

'Oh shit!' says Steve. 'I *knew* I should have come back sooner.'

'It's fine,' I say quickly. 'He tried to get over the fence from Eileen's garden - but she caught him at it and gave him a piece of her mind!'

'Was Eileen okay?' he asks.

'Okay?' I laugh. 'As far as I can tell, she had a brilliant time sending him away with a flea in his ear! She's been on house-watch for me ever since - and nothing sneaks past Eileen.'

'But you still needed the chair,' sighs Steve.

'I know it's stupid,' I shrug, 'but I really don't want to risk turning around and finding him in here with me!'

'I'm sorry,' he says.

'There's nothing for you to be sorry for,' I say with a shrug. 'It's not you who married the idiot.'

'Don't do that,' he says quickly.

'What?' I say.

'Don't blame yourself for someone else's bad behaviour.'

'I… don't?' It comes out as a question, because the moment he says it, it's like a final piece of this year's puzzle of misery slots into place. It's exactly what I've been doing all year - asking myself what I did wrong. What was it about me that made Colin behave like he did? The simple answer is – nothing. He behaves like he does because he is a dick.

'Okay,' I say quietly. 'I get it.'

Steve nods and, to his credit, he doesn't seem to feel the need to hammer the point home.

'Just for the record,' I say, 'Colin isn't dangerous or anything like that. He's just… Colin. A pain in my behind and I'm glad he's out of my life.'

'Noted,' says Steve. 'So... let's take a look at this door.'

'Great,' I nod. 'Then I can send the chair back where it belongs and let Eileen know she can stand down from house-watch duty!'

Steve yanks the chair out of the way.

'Blimey,' he says as he pulls the door open and a shower of rotten wood falls on him.

I wince. It's another job Colin was meant to do for the last... five or so years?

'This... might take a bit longer than expected,' says Steve.

'Sorry,' I mutter, cursing Colin in my head.

'It's no big deal,' he shrugs. 'Just needs a bit of filling.... And the hinges have sagged - see where that bit's split there? It's just going to need a bit of TLC before I fit the new lock.'

'Okay,' I say. 'I mean... if you've got time.'

Steve peers at his watch and frowns. 'I do... and I've got everything I need in the van...'

'But?' I prompt – because there's definitely a *but* coming.

'But – I promised Aunty Iris I'd grab some shopping for her,' he says.

'That's easy,' I say. 'Give me the list. If you're happy for me to abandon you here for a bit, I'll grab Iris's shopping while you fix my door.'

'Oh... that's really kind, but I can't ask you to do

that!' he says, ruffling his hair. I promptly get another blast of lemon.

'It's fine!' I say, doing my best to keep my voice as steady as possible. 'Fair division of labour - besides I could do with a bit of fresh air!'

CHAPTER FIFTEEN

ANGER IS LIKE A FINE WINE - IT'S BEST SERVED WITH A SIDE OF CHEESE, A GOOD LAUGH, AND MAYBE A NAP

Wrapping my coat tightly around me, I snuggle my chin down as far as it'll go into the collar. In the half an hour I've just spent watching Steve working his magic on my kitchen door, the weather's turned from cold to finger-numbingly freezing.

Ah well – this won't take long. I can get everything Iris needs from our local-ish corner shop – so I thought I'd walk instead of taking the car... but I'm already starting to doubt that choice. Maybe I should have asked Steve to borrow his ridiculous bobble hat! Actually – scratch that. He's already got me completely discombobulated with his over-protective reaction to my makeshift Colin-blockade. The last thing I need to do is surround myself with that scent of his!

It feels really weird leaving Steve and Arthur at the cottage – but I have to admit, Arthur looks completely at home on his duvet… and Steve's got his work cut out with that door! If it wasn't for the fact that Iris is expecting her nephew to deliver her shopping, I think I'd be inviting the friendly locksmith and his trusty companion to stay for dinner… in fact, I'm almost disappointed that won't be happening!

Pushing the heavy glass door open, I step into the little corner shop and breathe a sigh of relief as warm air swirls around me. I seriously need to get in the habit of wearing gloves when it's this cold!

I fumble as I reach for a basket, struggling to wrap my frozen, pink fingers around the handle.

'Holly?'

I turn to find my neighbour grinning at me.

'Hi Eileen!' I say with a huge smile - after all, she's my knight in shining house-coat!

'Sorry to abandon my post!' she says. 'I'll have my eyes on your back door before you know it. I just needed to pick up a few bits before the Christmas vultures arrive and clear the place out!'

I glance into her basket. There's a handful of basics - sliced bread, a couple of tins of soup and a can of peach halves in syrup.

'Well,' I say, 'you'll be pleased to know that you can abandon your post permanently. Steve the locksmith is back at the cottage right now, fitting a new lock.'

'Oh - shame!' laughs Eileen 'I've rather enjoyed playing security guard for you. I managed to push one of my armchairs over to the window, and I've got my binoculars on the sill - and a good selection of snacks. I find mint humbugs help a lot when you're on surveillance!'

'You're amazing!' I say, trying not to giggle at the mental image she's just painted. 'Thank you.'

'Any time,' says Eileen, 'it's been fun! Right... I'm going to have to press on with this shopping. I need to get a tin of corned beef for boxing day sandwiches... and then I'm all set.'

I raise my eyebrows, glancing down again at her rather scant basket.

'Eileen,' I say slowly as I walk with her towards the tins of cold meat, 'what are you up to for Christmas?'

'The usual,' she shrugs. 'A nice sandwich for lunch, maybe a tin of soup for tea... some bad TV and a nice long nap.'

Something twists in my stomach. There's no mention of any kind of company. I mean... I know I'm on my own, but that's different.

'Now then... don't you go looking at me like that!' she says stoutly.

'Like what?' I say, doing my best to look innocent.

'Like I told you my favourite hamster just died!' she says, grabbing a small tin of corned beef and checking the sell-by date.

'Have you got hamsters?' I say in surprise.

'Of course I don't, silly girl!' she hoots. 'You know what I mean. You're not to go feeling all sorry for me. I'm comfortable enough - and I'm not complaining!'

'Okay,' I nod. 'Sorry!'

She shrugs. 'Actually… I *am* complaining - but only about the awful television programmes. They always show repeats over Christmas. I mean, I'm sixty-seven - I've already seen them all!'

I grin at her. *Eighty*-seven years old and counting. This woman is my role model. Independent, trouble-some, and really rather wonderful.

'Thanks again for acting as security guard,' I say.

'My pleasure - now be off with you,' she says, making little shooing motions at me. 'Grab your shop-ping and get back to that handsome fellow in your kitchen!'

I grin at her. 'Merry Christmas, Eileen – for when it arrives!'

'You too, Holly my love!'

By the time I get back to the cottage, Steve's nearly done with the door. He's worked wonders while I've been away.

'See,' he says, grabbing the handle and swinging it open.

I wince, waiting for it to catch on the lino like it usually does – but not this time. It glides open silently.

'The frame's mended, and the hinges are fixed and oiled,' says Steve. 'I've just got to tighten up the lock, and then I'm done!'

'Thanks so much!' I say, kneeling down next to Arthur and stroking his silky ears. The big dog gives a huge yawn and seems to think about sitting up for a couple of seconds - before changing his mind and flopping back down onto his side.

I glance around the kitchen as Steve gets busy with a screwdriver. You'd think I'd been gone for hours. The shavings from the door have been swept up, the mess cleared away and most of the tools have already been placed carefully back into the toolbox. Whenever Colin grudgingly got around to a job, the place would look like a bomb had hit it for days.

I blow out a long breath. I *seriously* need to stop doing this. Colin's no longer part of my life… I need to make sure he's no longer part of my head either! It's time to move on…

'Hey - Holly?'

Steve's voice pulls me out of my thoughts.

'Sorry?' I say. Going by the look on his face, I think I might have missed something.

'You were miles away!' he laughs.

'Sorry!' I say again. *Focus woman!*

'It's fine,' he says with another one of his knee-jellifying smiles. 'It's just… I'm all done and… well…'

I watch as he turns a very cute shade of pink and then grabs his jacket from the back of one of the kitchen chairs.

'Are you going?' I say. I can't help the pang of disappointment.

'I am… but I was wondering…' he pauses and runs his fingers through his hair, looking weirdly nervous. 'I'm taking Aunty Iris's shopping over to her and we're having afternoon tea… she's baked fresh biscuits specially. I was wondering if you'd like to come too?'

'Oh!' I say, surprised. 'Erm… won't that be a lot for Iris - just out of the blue. And… maybe a bit awkward?'

'Nah!' he laughs. 'She's the one who suggested I invited you in the first place!'

'Really?' I say.

'Yeah! She thought it would be better coming from me because you're not my boss,' says Steve with a raised eyebrow. 'She didn't want you to feel awkward if you want to say no.

'Are you kidding me?' I say. 'I'm not going to say no - I'd love to come!'

'You would?' he says, breaking into a wide grin.

'Of course,' I laugh. 'There's no way I'm missing out on the chance to try Iris's biscuits!'

'Well then… shall we?' he says, holding out his hand to help me up from my spot next to Arthur's makeshift bed.

I grab his warm hand, and as his fingers curve around mine a tingle travels right up my arm. Then he gives a hefty tug and I fly to my feet and crash straight into him.

'Whoa!' he laughs as he steadies me.

Arthur gives a delighted *woof* from behind me, clearly thinking that it's some kind of game. I, however, can't say a thing. My crash-landing into Steve's chest released another puff of lemony, woody scent from his fleecy jacket, and it's as much as I can do not to snuggle into him and start sniffing his neck.

No Holly! No uninvited neck sniffing!

That would just be weird. Instead, I turn to Arthur.

'You coming to tea too, boy?' I say ruffling his ears as he scrambles to his feet.

'Are you kidding me?' laughs Steve, grabbing his toolbox before turning to check that the back door is properly secure. 'Iris is his number one fan - she spoils him rotten. I think she might actually be his one true love!'

CHAPTER SIXTEEN

IF LIFE GIVES YOU A RAINY DAY, PLAY IN THE PUDDLES OF YOUR RAGE. JUST REMEMBER TO WEAR WELLINGTON BOOTS

*I*t's quite nice being driven around... I could get used to it. The inside of Steve's van is clean and tidy... but blimey, he's got a lot of stuff packed in back there! The van is in a state of organised chaos, and there's barely an inch of spare room - though it does look like everything has its own special spot.

I glance over my shoulder at Arthur. I *think* he's just about forgiven me for usurping his position in the passenger seat next to Steve.

'Poor boy,' I laugh. 'You really didn't want to be back there, did you?'

'He's fine!' laughs Steve. 'Thank heavens for that duvet though. I think we would have been standing outside your cottage for hours without it.'

I laugh – though Steve's probably right. There was no getting Arthur out of the cottage without the duvet to begin with – and then the stand-off began. Arthur stood at the passenger door, stubbornly waiting for Steve to lift him up onto the front seat, with the duvet clamped firmly between his teeth. In the end, Steve managed to steal the thing and pop it into the back of the van. Arthur couldn't handle being separated from his new best friend and instantly hopped in after it without another complaint.

'Don't worry,' says Steve, 'I'll get it washed and back to you.'

'Nah - don't worry about that!' I say quickly. 'I think that's Arthur's duvet now. Anyway, there's no point it sitting in my airing cupboard doing nothing when it could be keeping Arthur comfy when he's out at work with you.'

'Well… Arthur says thanks,' says Steve.

'So - what's with all the boxes of Christmas decs back there?' I say, gawping at several large plastic boxes that are stacked in around Arthur's snoozing spot. From what I can see through the clear sides, the contents looks old and well-loved… the strands of tinsel a tad thin and tatty like most of mine.

'Aunty Iris likes to put her decorations up on Christmas Eve,' he says. 'So I've got them down from my loft, ready for action tomorrow. We're going to do it together.'

'Nice!' I say. 'I can't believe Christmas is nearly here! I'm not sure where December went if I'm honest.'

'I should imagine it's got something to do with

running a thriving business and packing up about a bajillion chocolates, from what Aunty Iris was saying,' says Steve, drawing to a halt as the traffic comes to a standstill and red brake lights flare around us in the afternoon gloom.

I wrap my arms around myself and, without missing a beat, Steve leans across and ramps up the van's heater, making sure the jets of hot air are pointed straight at me.

'Thanks!' I say with a little wiggle as my legs start to defrost a bit.

'Don't want you getting chilly,' says Steve, 'Aunty Iris will never forgive me.'

I grin at him. 'So… what have you got planned for Christmas?'

'Hot date with Aunty Iris!' he says.

'You guys are super close, aren't you?' I say.

Steve nods with a happy smile. 'Always have been! She's brilliant – I love spending Christmas with her. I mean, she much prefers a big crowd – she's used to cooking for dozens, not just two of us. I think she misses catering for the masses, but at least neither of us is on our own for Christmas, I guess.'

'Do you have a big family, then?' I ask lightly, hoping to distract him from asking me the same question. The last thing I want to do is tell him that's exactly how I'll be spending Christmas!

'Yeah – but most of them have relocated to Australia,' he says. 'The rest are scattered all over the country. That's why the pair of us keep each other company.'

'Bet she loves having you around,' I say.

'Not as much as I love being with her,' he grins. 'I just wish I could give her the kind of Christmas she loves, though – you know – bustling and full of people and laughter! You should see all her Christmas cards though – I swear she could paper the house with them.'

'Sounds like my office at Billingham's,' I smile, turning to stare out of the window as we set off again. The chilly fields are already glistening with early frost, and steam rises from the little river I can see winding away into the distance.

'Nearly there!' says Steve.

I know it's weird, but I'm a bit disappointed when we pull up outside Iris's house. There's something so cosy about being shut up in the van with Steve and Arthur in the dying light. Part of me isn't ready to break the spell...but then I spot Iris's grinning face in one of the windows.

'I think someone's noticed that we've arrived!' I grin, waving at Iris as Steve parks up.

'She'll have been on the lookout all afternoon!' he laughs. 'Come on - can't keep Arthur from his tickles.

The three of us pile out of the van, but Arthur's first to the front door – dragging his duvet with him.

Steve knocks lightly and suddenly I'm weirdly nervous. I've known Iris since before I can remember, but I've never been to her house before. This feels like… the start of something. Or maybe the end - I'm not sure which.

'Come in, come in!' cries Iris the minute she unfastens the safety chain from the front door.

Arthur barges into the warmth as Iris hugs Steve tightly before leading the way into the warm hallway. I step inside and close the door behind me. The hallway is lined with floor-to-ceiling strings of Christmas cards - and I gaze around, taking them all in.

'Told you so!' says Steve when he spots me staring at them. 'Cards from all over the world!'

'Plenty more through here in the living room,' says Iris, leaning around Steve's bulk. 'Come in and have a look! Steve – be a good lad and bring in the tea and biscuits. It's all ready in the kitchen.'

Steve nods and steps back to let me through. As I brush past him, I catch that wonderful lemony, woody scent again. Goosebumps instantly prickle along my arms, and I shiver and hurry in to join Iris.

'You weren't kidding about the cards!' I gasp as I step into the cosy living room. They're lined up on every available surface - along the mantlepiece, in front of the bookshelves, and even draped sideways over the edges of what must be dozens of framed photos.

'Wow!' I say, staring at the old photos. Most of them are black and white, though there are a few colour ones mixed in here and there – the soft tones making them look super vintagey.

I move closer to the largest one that's hanging in

pride of place, right over the mantlepiece. Sure enough, I recognise the front of Billingham's. There's a group of people gathered in front of the doors, all grinning into the camera.

'There's you!' says Iris, coming to stand next to me and pointing out a little girl right at the front.

I can't be more than three years old. I'm wearing a little party dress and Gramps is standing behind me with his hands resting on my shoulders. We're surrounded by Billingham's staff - and though I wouldn't necessarily have recognised myself - I spot several familiar faces.

'What was this?' I say. 'Everyone's so dressed up!'

'Billingham's Christmas party!' says Iris, her eyes lighting up. 'This one's always been one of my favourites. That one over there shows the inside from the same year!'

I turn to have a look at it. Sure enough, there are all the long packing tables we still use - but they've been arranged in a huge square. Everything else has been cleared aside, and the tables are set with a feast. Whoever took the photograph has managed to capture so much joy - paper hats, turkey, and smiles abound.

'This one's my favourite,' says Steve reappearing with a tray. He sets it carefully down on the table and then points at a photograph near the door. I head over to take a closer look.

My Nan and Gramps must be somewhere in their late twenties in this one. They're sitting side-by-side on a bench outside Billingham's. There are about a dozen women cosied in around them - faces pressed in close. One young stunner is lying on her side in front of Nan and Gramps's feet, a huge grin on her face.

'That's me at the front!' says Iris, coming to stand next to me.

'You?' I gasp. 'Oh Iris, look at you - what an amazing photo!'

'And that looker with her cheek pressed right up against your Nan's is Doris.'

'No way!' I laugh.

'Oh yes,' says Iris. 'Thick as thieves, those two. And that's Edna pretending to give Alf a kiss.'

I grin. We're surrounded by decades of Billingham's history... and it suddenly hits me just how much Gramps's factory - *my* factory - means to Iris... and probably most of the other Angels too.

'I'm so glad you've taken over, Holly,' she says, grabbing my hand and giving it an unexpectedly tight squeeze. 'It's just what Alf would have wanted. It's just... right.'

'Well... I'll do my best,' I say, my voice suddenly tight.

'You don't need to go worrying about that,' says Iris, turning a smile on me. 'You're already doing a grand job, and I bet next year will be even better – you'll have a chance to get your feet underneath you properly.'

I swallow and nod. I'll be free of Colin at last – I

think that's what she means, though I'm grateful she doesn't actually say it out loud.

'Milk, Holly?' says Steve.

I turn and he winks at me – making my stomach flip. I've got a feeling he's coming to my rescue by changing the subject and I'm super grateful. I could do without turning into a blubbering mess again this afternoon.

'Yes please!' I say.

'Don't miss the biscuits,' says Steve.

'I baked Steve's favourites,' says Iris. 'I do hope you like ginger, Holly?'

I nod and take one from the beautifully arranged plate she's holding out towards me. While the other two add milk to their cups, I nibble at it... if it's disgusting, I'll just have to slip it in my pocket or something.

'WOW...' I gasp. 'Iris?!'

'You okay there?' says Steve with a knowing grin.

I nod at him, but I can't say anything, I'm too busy taking another bite and letting out a loud - ever so slightly embarrassing - groan of pleasure.

'Told you so!' chuckles Steve. 'She'll ruin shop-bought biscuits for you too if you're not careful!'

'Oh good. I'm glad you like them!' says Iris. She's clearly trying to play it cool, but she's gone rosy pink and is smiling from ear to ear. 'Thank you for coming over, Holly - having you here like this really is the most wonderful Christmas present!'

I know it's a bit daft, but I feel weirdly nervous when Steve disappears to take Arthur out for a walk, leaving me alone with Iris.

'I don't suppose you fancy a peep at my photo albums, do you?' says Iris, looking excited. 'Seeing as you like the framed ones so much. I've got a pretty good collection from Billingham's over the years… and there's one album in particular that's got all the Christmas parties.'

'I'd love to!' I gasp. 'Until you showed me that one on the wall, I'd forgotten about the parties. They were good, weren't they?'

'Good?' says Iris, bending low as she opens a cupboard and chooses a heavy old tartan-covered album from the stack inside. 'They were an institution. All of us together on Christmas day - children running riot back in the day - extended families - boyfriends, husbands, wives… it was a riot!'

She settles herself next to me on the old sofa and places the album on my lap. I flip its cover open and stare down at the first page. Each photograph is accompanied by a note of the year and a list of names in Iris's familiar, elegant hand.

'This is amazing!' I say, turning the pages slowly and searching for my grandparents' faces in each photo, watching as the years soften their smiles and then add wrinkles.

I'm about halfway through when I pause. With the turn of a page, my nan has disappeared. It might be my imagination, but Gramps's smile looks slightly hollow. Iris rests her hand on my arm.

'He loved your nan so much,' she says softly.

'I know,' I say. 'It was hard not to.'

I stare at the photos in front of me, willing my hot eyes to behave themselves. Nan passed away so long ago now - but I still miss her.

'I can't imagine how he must have felt - being without her for all those years,' I sigh.

'I think that's why he never retired,' says Iris. 'Billingham's kept him going.'

'No,' I say. 'His Angels are what kept him going.'

Iris shrugs. 'That's what families do. And of course, Doris really stepped up to help him... and then you joined us.'

I nod and turn over a few more pages in the album.

'It's a shame the Christmas parties petered out,' she sighs. 'They really were quite something, you know!'

'I remember,' I say quietly. 'A few of them, at least.'

Obviously, I didn't go to them all. My day with Nan and Gramps was usually Christmas Eve- and then I'd spend Christmas day with mum and dad... but some years the three of us would descend on Billingham's too.

'There's nothing like preparing Christmas dinner for that many people!' says Iris. 'It was so much fun! These days, it's just me and Steve - and Arthur of course! I love them dearly... but it's definitely not the same as being surrounded by twenty or more chatter-boxes as they tuck into the meal you've just prepared!'

I bite my lip. An idea is busy prodding me in the brain... but there's no way I'm saying a thing about it to Iris until I've had the chance to think it through properly.

'Hey, Iris... can I ask a favour?' I say, closing the album softly.

'Anything!' says Iris, looking delighted.

'May I borrow this for a few days?' I say, stroking the album's tartan cover. 'I'd love to have another look through it – and maybe snap a couple of copies of the photos with my phone, if you wouldn't mind?'

'Of course,' says Iris. 'And maybe you'll come around for tea again – and we can look through some of the others.'

'I'd love that,' I say, smiling at her. 'Thanks Iris.'

'Ah, you're a good girl, Holly Billingham,' she says. 'You always were.'

CHAPTER SEVENTEEN

ANGER IS LIKE A GPS FOR YOUR SOUL. IT'S JUST TRYING TO REROUTE YOU TO A HAPPIER DESTINATION

'Thank you so much for the lift!' I say as Steve pulls up outside the cottage.

'Pleasure's all mine!' he says. 'You made Iris's day, you know?'

'How?' I laugh, 'by swooning over her baking.

'That... and for coming over in the first place,' he says seriously. 'Alf meant the world to her, and I know she misses him terribly. All this worry about whether Billingham's was going to close or not has been really hard on her.'

'I'm sorry-' I start, but Steve shakes his head.

'Don't be - it's not your fault. Or at least not something to apologise for... or... erm... just one of those things...?' he takes a breath and ruffles his hair. 'This is coming out all wrong. I just meant to say - well - it just means a lot that you've stepped into Alf's shoes.'

'I'll never be able to do that,' I say quietly.

'Maybe not - but you're a Billingham again, Holly,' he says with a smile, 'and it shows, it really does.'

I smile at him, but I'm not really sure what to say. I think I'd better get out of this van pronto before the urge to hurl myself into his lap and kiss his face off gets any stronger.

'Night night, Arthur,' I say, turning to the snoozing mound of dog in the back. All I get in return is a snuffling snore from the depths of the duvet.

I'm only a couple of steps up the path when Steve calls my name.

'Yeah?' I say, turning back to him. He's wound down the window of the van.

'Come here a sec?'

His voice makes my heart do a backflip and I feel like I'm gulping in the chilly evening air, trying to catch my breath. I watch for a moment as the wind ruffles his hair - and all I want to do is run my fingers through it.

Suddenly, the world is going in slow motion and I feel like I've landed in one of Linda's romcoms. Is he going to kiss me? I mean... this afternoon wasn't a date, was it? But... I'm not going to complain if that *is* his plan.

After what feels like forever - although it's probably just a matter of seconds - I'm standing next to the van again. I hope I'm not panting... but then, I wouldn't put it past me. I'm definitely having a hard time catching my breath and it's the kind of embarrassing thing I'd do!

Steve locks his eyes on my face and I squirm.

'Here,' he says quietly, reaching his hand out of the window.

I look at it in confusion for a long moment. Does he want me to hold his hand or something? It's at a bit of a weird angle... but...

I shoot my hand out before I can overthink it, and I'm just wrapping my fingers around his when I feel something hard and cold pressing into my palm.

'Oh!' I say.

Retreat! RETREAT!

Of *course* he wasn't trying to hold my hand through the window of a van - only a weirdo would think that!

'Your keys!' he says with a laugh that sounds more than a little bit awkward. 'For the back door?'

'Of course!' I say - as though it hadn't crossed my mind for a second it could be anything else. 'Cheers!' I add, stumbling back from the van as though I've been pushed. I give him the nerdiest of nerdy thumbs up – and promptly drop the keys into the mud.

Stooping down to retrieve them, I reappear feeling more than a little bit pink around the edges. Honestly... could I *be* any more awkward? Poor bloke!

'I'd better go,' he says. 'Thanks for a lovely afternoon.'

'Yeah - you too,' I say quickly. 'I mean - cheers!'

Urgh - shut up, Holly!

'I mean it,' says Steve, smiling at me warmly. 'That meant a lot to Iris!'

'Actually - me too,' I say, breathing a sigh of relief that I manage to sound vaguely normal. 'I promise I'll get the album back to her before too long.'

I hoik the tote bag Iris lent me more securely onto my shoulder. I can't wait to peruse her Billingham's Christmas album again. I'm not sure why, but it feels like it holds some kind of key. Perhaps I just want to spend a bit more time soaking up all those years of happiness preserved between the pages.

'See you soon, Holly!' says Steve, putting the van in reverse.

I give him the thumbs up again – just to make sure my title of Queen Nerd of the Galaxy is well and truly fixed in stone.

Turning back towards the cottage, I catch a tiny twitch at Eileen's curtains next door. I can't see if she's still there, but I grin and wave - just in case she's still watching. No doubt I'll be facing the inquisition next time I see her... but I don't mind in the slightest. I'm sure she'll get a giggle out of me making a prat of myself – if she hasn't already!

Letting myself inside, I can't help but notice that the cottage - which is usually so cosy and welcoming - feels a bit cold and quiet after the warmth and chatter of Iris's house. I head straight through to the kitchen, flicking on all the lights as I go, and then turn on the radio for some Christmas music for good measure.

There - much better!

I pop the kettle on to boil and then glance over at the back door with its posh new lock. I can't resist testing it out... just to check! Like a toddler, I open and close it several times, marvelling at how smooth it is on its new hinges before closing it firmly and flipping the latch. It gives a reassuring click. I give it a good, hefty tug – and then smile. I definitely won't be needing a chair against it as backup tonight! Hopefully, I'll be able to sleep a bit better knowing there's no chance of Colin letting himself in!

Actually – scrap that. I might not spend the night worrying about my ex-husband, but I've got a feeling something else is going to be busy keeping me awake... or *someone*, I should say!

The image of me trying to hold Steve's hand just now pops back into my head, and I do a fidgety little dance on the spot.

'Gah - soooo embarrassing!' I mutter.

But... I don't need to worry about it, do I? Steve's not Colin. He's kind, he's funny – and from what I've seen of him so far, he's man enough to deal with me being... well... me.

I sip my tea and turn to stare at the spot where Arthur was curled up on his duvet just a few hours ago. I'd give anything to be able to give him a hug right now… though if I'm honest - I'd like one from Steve even more.

'Pull yourself together!' I laugh, cranking the volume up on the Christmas carols in an attempt to stop myself from feeling so alone.

Wait… what was that?

I turn the dial back down again - practically muting the tune.

Bbrring BBRRING!

I thought so. It's my landline.

Puffing air into my cheeks, I freeze on the spot and for a brief moment, I consider ignoring it.

But it could be important…

Or an emergency… or…

I dash through to the living room and grab the receiver.

'Holly, it's Marcia!'

I *really* need to get better at the whole ignoring-the-phone thing!

'Don't hang up!' she adds quickly.

I raise my eyebrows. I mean, as tempting as that sounds, I'm not sure I'm physically capable of doing it… unless it happens to be Colin on the other end of the line of course!

'Hi,' I say with a sigh that's most definitely audible. 'Look it's not a great time.'

Seriously though, when is it *ever* a good time to have your ex-husband's new girlfriend calling you?

'I won't keep you long,' she says.

I frown. Marcia sounds… different. Less snitty and snarky and more… like she's trying to be nice? I'm instantly on my guard. Call me suspicious, but… *why?*

'What is it?' I say, narrowing my eyes.

'Is Colin with you?' she says, lowering her voice as though he might be able to hear what she's saying.

'No, Marcia. Colin isn't with me,' I huff. 'Plus - though this might be really hard for you to grasp - I have absolutely no interest in my very soon-to-be ex-husband's whereabouts. He's my ex for a reason!'

I manage to stop short of pointing out that *she* is a big part of that reason.

'I know,' she says, sounding almost sad. 'I'm so sorry, Holly.'

I raise my eyebrows. 'Are you okay?' I say… because I *clearly* just can't stop myself.

'I will be now he's gone,' she says.

'Who's gone?' I say.

'Colin,' she says, and I can practically hear the eyeroll. 'Look - I just wanted to give you the heads up that he's probably on his way over to you.'

'But… why?'

'He told you we'd split up the other night, right?' she says.

'Yes - but I though he was talking through his back-side?' I say.

'He was,' says Marcia. 'But I've just chucked him out… for good this time. I found out he's sleeping with someone else…'

'Yeah - well, it's not me!' I say.

'I know that,' says Marcia quickly. 'And when I said I'm sorry... I mean for everything! I get it... at least a little bit.'

'Get it?' I say. 'Get what?'

'How you felt last Christmas,' she says. 'I'm sorry for my part in what he did to you. I hope you believe me.'

'I *guess* I do...' I say. Because, to be honest, the usually ballsy Marcia sounds more than a little bit broken.

'This doesn't excuse anything, but he told me you guys were separated back then,' she says.

'Yeah? Well, we weren't,' I say. 'But... well... I guess that's not your fault,' I add.

'Thanks, Holly,' she says. 'That's really kind of you.'

'Don't get used to it!' I huff. 'It's Christmas... I'm clearly feeling sentimental.'

'That's why I wanted to warn you!' she says quickly.

'What do you mean?' I say.

'I know how soft you are - and I don't mean that in a bad way!' she adds quickly, clearly sensing I'm already gearing up to bite her head off. 'I mean - you're nice.'

'So?'

'So Colin's on his way to your place,' she says. 'I chucked him out... and I guess he figures he can just... crawl back.'

'We'll see about that,' I huff.

'You deserve better!' says Marcia.

'Yeah - well - so do you,' I say, surprised to find that I mean it. 'Thanks for the heads up.'

'No worries,' she mumbles.

'Hey Marcia?' I say, this time with a proper smile on my face.

'Yeah?'

'Merry Christmas!'

CHAPTER EIGHTEEN

CHANNEL YOUR INNER REINDEER - STAND TALL, BE FABULOUS – AND IF SOMEONE ANNOYS YOU, GIVE THEM A PROD WITH YOUR ANTLERS

I've barely had the chance to check that both doors are securely locked and the new chains Steve installed for me are in place when the landline rings again. I roll my eyes. Given Marcia's warning, there's only one person that can be... and I'm not really in the mood.

I pad back into the living room and stare at the phone. I've got no interest in talking to Colin... especially after the lovely day I've just had. I let it ring as I stare around the room, willing the twinkling tree lights and tinsel to calm my jangled nerves.

Of course... if it *is* Colin and I *don't* answer... it's more likely that he'll just turn up at the front door. New locks or not – I really don't want a scene.

I lunge for the handset.

'What?' I growl, sounding more than a little bit like a pissed-off she-wolf.

There's silence on the other end for a long moment, and I cringe. What if I'm wrong and it's not Colin? What if I've just managed to seriously offend one of Alf's Angels?!

'Hello?' I say again, this time in a more human tone.

'Oh, it *is* you,' comes a huffy voice. 'I thought I'd got the wrong number.'

'Colin,' I sigh. 'What?'

'Don't say *what* like that,' he says.

I'm about to tell him I can say whatever I like - however I like, when I just shrug instead. I've had enough of the games and he doesn't deserve any of my energy.

'I'm in a taxi on my way over,' he says. 'Marcia and I are having a few problems.'

I roll my eyes. The man certainly has an interesting way of spinning things. I need to put a stop to this now... before he's hammering on the door, expecting to be let in.

'Colin, I-'

'I'll only stay a few days,' he says, cutting across me forcefully. 'I just need to get my head on straight. I'll sleep on the couch - unless you'd prefer it if I didn't.'

'I really don't-' I start

'Okay, that's settled,' he says quickly. 'You take the sofa and I'll take our bed. I won't be long – I need you to pay for the taxi when I get there - I'm a bit short of cash at the minute!'

I swear, if my jaw drops open any further, it's going to dislocate itself. I must look like I'm trying to re-enact The Scream right now!

'I hope you've got my spare keys cut,' he chunters on, 'otherwise it's going to be really inconvenient for me while I'm staying. I mean… I don't want to be a prisoner in the place do I?'

The thought of Colin behind bars gives me a momentary smile of satisfaction. If only they locked people up for simply being pure, solid-gold idiots!

'Oh - and I need you to lay some clothes out for me,' he says. 'I need to change.'

'What…?' Maybe I'm asleep and this is just a weird dream… it's definitely getting surreal enough!

'Marcia… erm… spilt some wine,' he mutters. 'I'm sure I left a couple of shirts in the wardrobe. Just iron one and lay it out on the bed. Actually, thinking about the bed – you need to change the sheets before I get there. I don't want to sleep in yours, that would just be weird.'

I've just crossed some kind of invisible barrier from mildly-confused to downright angry. My chest is tight and I've suddenly got this raging need to break something. I swear there's steam pouring out of the top of my head.

'It looks like we're going to be having Christmas dinner together after all,' he says. I can hear the wide, satisfied grin on his face.

Christmas dinner together? That would be a bad, bad plan!

There's no way I should be allowed anywhere near him and a bunch of blunt spoons at the same time – otherwise, I might just be tempted to remove his kneecaps.

'I don't want roast potatoes though, Holly!' he says. 'Yours are always really dry... I want dauphinoise. You'd better have some decent booze in the house, though I guess you could go out and get some tomorrow.'

At long last, he pauses to take a breath.

The steam pouring out of my head has now gone all red-mist on me, and suddenly Doris's words from her little lesson on how to be angry come back to me.

'Holly? Are you still there?' he demands.

'Oh - I'm here, alright,' I growl.

'What's up, Holly Berry?' he chuckles.

Something inside my usually soft, kind, chilled-out brain snaps.

'Listen closely,' I say in a dangerous whisper. 'I won't be paying for your taxi. I won't be making up *any* kind of bed for you. I won't be laying out your clothes or buying booze or roasting potatoes...'

'Dauphinois!' he says. 'Jeez – you never listen.'

'There won't be *any* kind of potatoes,' I rumble, 'because you won't be here.'

'But where am I meant to go?' he whines. 'I'm ten minutes away, and-'

Oh no you don't, it's my turn!

'I don't really care, Colin,' I say, and a hysterical bubble of laughter slips out with the words. 'If you come here - the doorstep is as far as you're getting.'

'But-'

'ENOUGH!' I roar.

He goes very, *very* quiet.

'I've had enough,' I repeat – just in case he missed it the first time. 'You are no longer part of my life. You're history - once and for all. No ifs, buts or maybes. I *know* you. I've believed you before… and I *know* you. Frankly - I've wasted enough of my life on your rubbish.'

'But Holly-!'

'We're done. Don't come here, Colin. You aren't welcome,' I say. 'Oh… and I guess I should warn you that Eileen said she'd call the police next time she spots you anywhere near the cottage.'

'Holly! I don't-'

'Goodbye, Colin,' I say.

Before he can say anything else, I place the receiver gently into the cradle.

In the twinkling silence that surrounds me, I take several long, deep breaths. Something feels different… like… I'm finally done with it all. I just wish I'd had the balls to do that a very long time ago. I guess I just needed my cheerleading squad in place – my team of Angels.

I've been so caught up with Colin and his silly little

games that I almost lost sight of what's really important... people like Iris and Doris and the rest of the Angels. Wonderful neighbours like Eileen. New friends like Steve and Arthur. People who *really* love and care for me – just as I am.

I head over to the window and peep outside, half expecting to see a taxi pulling up in the driveway - but there's nothing other than the deep, velvety darkness.

———

Shuffling over onto my back, I drag the duvet right up to my nose and stare at the ceiling. I should be fast asleep, but just like I prophesied, I've been busy trying to throttle myself with my bedding for hours – turning over and over again as my restless brain refuses to switch off.

I listen to the old cottage, creaking in the wind. It's really wild out there I'm cocooned in the cosy warmth of my bed – safe and sound behind my new locks. Nothing's going to disturb me.

I blow out a frustrated sound and turn onto one side, yanking the duvet with me as my mind still gallops through a fast replay of the last few days.

After hanging up on Colin, I decided to unplug the phone completely, figuring that I deserved some peace and quiet. At long last – I think I've finally learned that it's up to me to make sure that happens. I have no idea what happened to Colin in the end - not that I care anyway.

Still – I can't say I'm not glad that there haven't been any unwanted visitors banging on the door. I'm not sure if it's because the message has finally sunk in, or he's simply too scared to face Eileen. Either way, it made for a decidedly peaceful evening. I made the most of it, curled up on the sofa in front of the Christmas tree - with a sherry in one hand and Iris's photo album open on my lap.

And yet here I am… wide awake.

It's not Colin that's bothering me, though… or even thoughts of Steve, though he's definitely been an unexpected high point these past few days.

Suddenly… I recognise this feeling. It's the night before Christmas Eve… and I'm a little girl again, excited to go to Nan and Gramp's house in the morning. Excited – just because it's my favourite time of the year.

I smile sadly into the darkness. If only Nan and Gramps were still here.

Don't be daft, my girl – nothing stays the same forever – get on with it!

I laugh out loud as Gramps's voice rings out at full volume inside my head. It's the same thing he told me when I was decorating the tree… and of course, he's right – as always. I might not be a little kid anymore, but it's my favourite time of year - and this year I'm free to enjoy it without the weight of someone else's behaviour weighing me down. There's an entire, tinsel-wrapped world out there just waiting for me.

I turn over again, this time onto my stomach. The duvet twists around with me and I giggle and wriggle, slapping my feet up and down as I squirm with excitement. I seek out the cold edges of the bed with my feet in an attempt to shock myself out of this giddiness. Something's got right under my skin.

I close my eyes, welcoming the dark softness of my pillows pressing against my face. My mind settles on Iris's photo albums with its years of wonderful Christmas parties at Billingham's.

I flip over again, this time sitting bolt upright in bed.

'Don't be an idiot!' I whisper. 'It's impossible!'

I've already examined and scrapped the seed of an idea that started in Iris's living room… but clearly, some ideas are way more stubborn than I give them credit for. *This* is what's been holding my sleep hostage, isn't it?

I sit still, grinning like an idiot into the darkness. It *might* just be possible… as long as I can round up a bit of help.

'What a merry Christmas that would be!'

I grab my phone. There's no time like the present!

'Or maybe not!' I laugh. According to my phone, it's only just gone three a.m. Somehow, I don't think I'm going to be on the receiving end of much Christmas cheer if I start making phone calls right now!

'Go to sleep, idiot!' I mutter to myself and flop back down onto the pillows with an extravagant sigh. I close my eyes and grin into the darkness as I will sleep to come and club me over the head.

CHAPTER NINETEEN

ANGER IS LIKE A MIS-DELIVERED PRESENT. IT'S NOT WHAT YOU WANTED, BUT IT'S HERE

'So... you don't think it's a bad idea?' I say, staring from Steve to Iris and then back again.

We're all sitting in my living room. Iris and I are cosied up side-by-side on the sofa and Steve is lounging in the armchair across from us, looking so comfortable that it's hard to believe he hasn't been enjoying that spot for years. Arthur snuffles around in his duvet, the little jingle-bells on his blue and white snowflake jumper tinkling as he seeks out any Rich Tea crumbs he might have missed.

Iris doesn't say anything, she just stares at me with wide eyes.

'Give her a sec,' laughs Steve. 'I think she's in shock!'

He grins at me and I smile nervously back. I know I should feel bad for interrupting their Christmas Eve – but I'm just too excited. I called Steve's mobile the minute I woke up and the clock told me it was a vaguely acceptable time of day… not that *any* time of day is really acceptable on Christmas Eve - let's face it.

After convincing him that I didn't need saving from some kind of Colin-related emergency, he agreed to scoop up Iris and then join me for a morning cuppa so that I could regale them both with my mad idea in person.

'You really mean it?' says Iris. Her eyes shine with excitement and I can see that my plan is finally sinking in.

I nod.

'Is this why you wanted to borrow that album?' chuckles Steve.

'Partly…' I say.

'Were you up all night studying it?' says Iris, studying my face.

'Not *all* night,' I say, doing my best to fight back a yawn and failing miserably. 'But… you don't think it's a totally mad idea?'

'Not *totally!*' says Iris, reaching out and squeezing my hand.

'What about you?' I say, turning to Steve. He instantly holds his hands up in surrender.

'I don't think I get any kind of say in the matter - I don't work at Billingham's.'

'No!' says Iris. 'But this is your Christmas too… and it's going to take a lot of work.'

'Yeah,' I nod, 'and I'm going to rope you in if we go ahead!'

'Well then - consider me well and truly roped in!' he says with an easy shrug. 'I'm up for it - I think it's a wonderful idea.'

'Well then - let's do it!' I say, my stomach squeezing with excitement.

'Fancy…' says Iris, with a little wriggle and a dreamy look on her face. 'The return of Christmas at Billingham's! Ooh – your Gramps would be so excited!'

'So… what do we need to do to make this happen,' says Steve, looking resigned to his fate.

'First things first,' says Iris, 'you're going to need to get Doris on board as well, then she'll be able to help us get hold of everyone else. I'll call her as soon as I get home if you'd like?'

'Let's call her now!' I say. 'I don't want to wait. I've got her number in here…'

I grab my mobile, but Iris shakes her head and laughs. 'I know her number, dear. How about you pop the kettle on for more tea?'

'Okay!' I say, bouncing to my feet.

'If Doris is on board, then it's all systems go!' says Iris. 'Are you ready?

'So ready!' I practically squeak.

Steve gets to his feet too and pats his knees. 'Come on, Arthur old boy - I think you need a walk. I've got a feeling things are about to get very busy around here!'

I'm about to make a break for the kitchen when Iris stops me.

'Holly love,' she says, 'before I dial, what *exactly* am I saying to Doris?'

'That we've got a plan to have a Christmas dinner and a party at Billingham's... tomorrow!' I can't keep the ridiculous grin off my face as I say it. 'We're going to invite all the Angels - staff, extended family, friends. Everyone is welcome - just like when Nan and Gramps used to do it.'

'Right!' says Iris.

'Fingers crossed she's up for it!' I add. 'Then... I guess we'll need a rough idea of how many people might turn up - and then we'll raid the shops to see what we can get our hands on this late in the game!'

Iris nods slowly, taking it all in... and then something changes. I see her straighten in her seat and pull herself together. She's got her game-face on and there's no stopping her now!

I point her towards the phone and then head through to the kitchen with Steve and Arthur at my heels.

'Thank you!' he whispers.

'What for?' I say in surprise, turning to find him a bit closer than expected. I smile up at him... and only just manage to stop myself from reaching up and running a finger over his stubble.

Blimey - what's got into me?!

He grins down at me, and for a second I wonder if

he's doing that mind-reading thing again. I pull in a ragged breath. I must be more sleep-deprived than I thought because I swear it looks like he's about to kiss me.

Oh my... he is!

Steve's eyes are locked with mine, and even as the sound of Iris babbling away to Doris drifts through from the next room, he reaches out and brushes his fingertips lightly over my cheek.

'Wow!' Steve steps back abruptly, as though I've just stung him.

'Wha-? Oof!' I laugh. I go from confused to bowled over - quite literally - as a big, hairy gooseberry in the shape of Arthur shoves his way between us.

'Okay - sorry about my needy hound!' he laughs, looking decidedly awkward and more than a little pink all of a sudden.

I grin at him and shrug... but the moment is most definitely over.

'Tea?' I say lightly, determined not to let this become a "thing".

'Nah... thanks!' He shakes his head. 'I think I'd better get on and walk this one before he disgraces himself any further. Then... I'll be at your service for any mad party planning required - okay?'

'Are you sure?' I say. 'I mean... I don't want to ruin your plans.'

'Holly - stop!' he laughs. 'You're not ruining

anything. I've got a feeling this is going to be a Christmas to remember.'

The look on his face takes my breath away and, for a moment, the entire room stills as he holds my eye.

'Cooee?' Iris calls from the next room. 'Holly, you there?'

'See you in a bit,' says Steve with a small smile. Then he clips Arthur's lead onto his collar and heads back through the house towards the front door.

'Two secs, Iris!' I call back. 'I'm just making that tea.

'That's okay!'

I jump as she materialises right beside me. She's looking flushed and excited.

'What did Doris say?' I ask, piling the pot, cups and sugar bowl onto a tray.

'She...'

'Hated it?' I say, jumping in.

'Hush!' laughs Iris. 'She actually... what's the best word, here?' she pauses a moment and cocks her head. 'She *squealed*.'

'Doris?' I laugh. 'Are you sure it was her and not an impostor?'

'Definitely her!' says Iris, jiggling up and down on the balls of her feet. 'Bring that tea through - we've got a lot to do!'

I follow her back into the living room, place the tray carefully down on the coffee table and start to pour. I've got a feeling my guest is far too excited to be able to do it without upending the teapot all over the carpet.

'Doris is going to start ringing around straight away. We've divided everyone up between us - and I'm going to call the other half. So I'll have this cuppa and then get Steve to drive me home so I can get on with it,' she says, taking her cup with a grateful nod. 'Where are the boys, anyway?'

'Steve's just taken Arthur out for that walk,' I say, doing my best not to think about his strong fingers tracing my jaw for that brief moment.

'Drat,' says Iris. 'I was hoping to make a start straight away.'

'Call from here!' I say. 'There's no need to head home.'

'Are you sure?' says Iris.

'Of course,' I say quickly. 'I'm sure I've got a note of everyone's numbers somewhere.'

'No need for that,' says Iris, taking a fortifying sip of tea. 'I've had everyone's numbers memorised since my second week at Billingham's. I might be getting on a bit - but I've still got it all going on up here!' she taps her temple.

'Okay - I'm officially impressed!' I say.

'That's how we did it back in the day,' Iris shrugs. 'None of these new-fangled contraptions. Nice hand-writing and good brains were the order of the day.'

'Just as well!' I laugh. 'It would probably take me an age to find my little black book of telephone numbers anyway. So… did you and Doris manage to figure out a rough number of people we might be expecting? I'm going to need to hit the shops asap - Steve said he'd give me a hand!'

'Yup, I did!'

Both of us jump in unison and we turn towards the doorway only to find Steve standing there. Arthur pushes past him and heads straight for his duvet in front of the Christmas tree.

'That was quick!' I say, not quite meeting his eye.

'It's cold out there,' he shrugs. 'Arthur started to protest about having to go out at all, so we paid a visit to the big oak tree at the end of the road and then turned around and came straight back. Besides… I don't want to miss out on the fun!'

'Good lad!' says Iris approvingly, though I'm not entirely sure whether means Steve or Arthur.

'So…' I say, 'let's catch you up - Doris is in!'

'Yay!' says Steve, throwing himself back into the armchair across from Iris and helping himself to a cup of tea from the pot.

'Iris and Doris have come up with a rough number of people we're going to shop for,' I add.

'Which is?' asks Steve, curiously.

'Well - Doris reckons if all the Angels come - which is almost guaranteed - we might be looking at about twenty. Maybe more.'

'Wow!' I say, my eyes widening. 'I mean… do you *really* think they'll all come at such short notice?'

'Holly,' says Iris, catching my eye and giving me a serious look, 'here's the thing you need to understand. None of us is as young as we once were. Most of us are on our own, or it's just the old codger at home. Not everyone's lucky enough to have youngsters like my Steve here willing to keep them company.'

Steve goes to say something but Iris shoots him a look and he promptly shuts his mouth.

'Holly - we're all best friends. Billingham's is our home.' She pauses to take a long, excited breath. 'This is going to be the best Christmas ever. Just promise me you won't try to do everything on your own – we'll want to help – that's half the fun!'

'I promise!' I laugh as relief floods through me. It's only just dawning on me what a huge undertaking catering for twenty or more people at the last minute is going to be.

'Good,' says Iris, patting my knee.

'What about chairs and tables… and cups and plates and cutlery?' says Steve, cocking his head. 'That's a lot of stuff to find!'

'Oh - we've already got all that,' says Iris with a shrug. 'We used it every Christmas - and whenever Alf decided he fancied a party - which was pretty often if I'm honest!'

'But… where is it all?' I ask with a frown. 'I can't remember seeing anything like that at Billingham's. Is it in storage or something?'

'It's all tucked away in the old kitchen,' she says.

'There are some extra folding chairs in there some-where too, and we used to use the big packing tables for the meal. We just covered them with some pretty cloths - and then went from there.'

'The kitchen?' I say. It's a space that is basically used as a glorified cupboard these days, and there's so much stuff packed into it we're going to have our hands full before we can actually cook anything in there!

'Everything will need a good wash, of course,' Iris continues, completely unperturbed. 'It hasn't been used in years. Still, nothing a good scrub in some hot, soapy water won't sort out.'

This job is getting bigger by the second... but there's no backing out now, even if I wanted to. Iris is practically vibrating with excitement!

'Right then, you two,' she says. 'You need to hit the shops - and I need to make these calls.'

'Okay,' I say with a nod. 'Two things before we get going.'

'Which are?' says Iris.

I grin. So much for the quiet woman I thought I knew. Iris Bennet is a troublesome firecracker.

'Do you know Eileen next door?' I say, thinking about her meagre shopping basket of soup and sliced bread.

'Of course!' says Iris. 'We're old friends. We used to go to whist club together until it closed down. I think she knows nearly everyone at Billingham's. Why do you ask?'

'I'd like to invite her as my guest,' I say.

'Lovely idea,' says Iris with a brisk nod. 'I'll add her to my list.'

'Can you... not tell her?' I add. 'I'd like it to be a surprise.'

'Of course! Though it might be an idea to let her know you're planning to kidnap her on Christmas day,' says Iris, cocking her head as she thinks about it. 'I'm all for a surprise, but us oldies *do* like a little bit of time to adjust to things. Just keep the part about where you're taking her secret.'

'Okay,' I grin. 'Good idea.'

'Now... what was the other thing? I've got a lot of calls to make you know!' she says with a smile.

'Can you help me make a list... before we go?' I say. 'As you're going to be head chef, I want to make sure we get everything you're going to need.'

Steve shoots me a warm smile and Iris pulls herself up, looking proud as punch.

'Ooh, head chef?' she says. 'Just wait until I tell the others that! But - good idea. Steve - fetch me some paper and I'll make a start.'

CHAPTER TWENTY

STRESSED SPELLED BACKWARD IS
DESSERTS. COINCIDENCE? I THINK NOT!
PASS THE PLUM PUDDING!

*S*teve was right – it *is* ridiculously cold out here. We've just spent ten minutes emptying the back of Steve's van and piling all his tools into my hallway so that we'll have enough room for everything on Iris's list.

'Right – that's the last of it,' he says, pulling my front door closed behind him. There's no point saying goodbye to Iris – she's already on phone call number five, and is deep in conversation in the Livingroom, with Arthur keeping her company.

'Ready? Says Steve. 'Got the list?'

I rummage around in my pocket, just to make sure. The thing's so long it's more like a scroll – and I haven't a hope of remembering even half of the items if I do manage to leave it behind.

'Got it!' I nod, clambering into the van. 'You realise there's a good chance we're not going to be able to get all of this,' I say, running my eyes down Iris's immaculate, loopy writing as Steve starts the engine and we wait for the van's blowers to kick in. 'I mean – it is Christmas Eve!'

'How about this,' says Steve. 'Let's start at the nearest, biggest shop - and go from there!'

'Good call!' I say with a nod. 'To the shops!'

'To the shops!' he cheers.

It's just as well we emptied the back of the van before we set off. I don't think I've ever seen such a huge haul of goodies in my life... and we're not even finished yet.

'Right... I think that's enough treats, sweets, fruit and veg,' I say as I watch Steve carefully stack the last crate of veggies into the back.

We gave up on the supermarkets after visiting the third one in a row. They were fine for the basics - but the vegetable aisles had been picked bare. I came very close to having a panic attack over the one and only withered carrot in the last one – but then Steve came to the rescue.

'Lucky you came!' I say, shooting him a wink.

'Yeah - I'm not sure all this would have fitted in that little car of yours!' he says, smiling at me before pushing the van door closed. It refuses to latch until he turns around and leans his entire weight against it.

'I didn't mean that,' I laugh. 'I had no idea this place even existed - it's brilliant.'

After removing the aforementioned sad carrot from my icy grip, Steve drove us to this tucked-away farmers' market in the next town. We've basically just emptied out three veggie stalls in a row, leaving a bunch of very happy stallholders in our wake.

'Right,' I say, 'we're nearly there... apart from meat. At this rate it might end up being a veggie Christmas... but I guess there are worse things in the world.'

Even as I say it, I've got a sneaking suspicion I might be facing a sea of disappointed faces if everyone has to sit down to a plate heaped with veg and stuffing for Christmas dinner.

'No fear of that,' says Steve, shooting me a cheeky wink that instantly makes my toes curl. 'I've got a plan... if you're willing to go on a little adventure.'

'Adventure?' I laugh, raising my eyebrows. 'What about Iris?'

'Oh - she'll be on the phone for hours,' chuckles Steve. 'I mean, let's face it - you've basically left her with the job of calling ten of her nearest and dearest best friends!'

'But... they all saw each other just yesterday!' I say.

'Right - so there's a *lot* to catch up on!' says Steve.

'Okay,' I laugh. 'As long as you're sure she won't mind that we've abandoned her at my place.'

'Are you kidding me?' he says. 'She won't even notice we're gone. Besides - she's got my mobile number in that noggin of hers if she needs us. You up for it, Billingham?'

I lock eyes with Steve, and there it is again, that intense *something* that seems to be brewing between us.

I swallow.

Our hairy gooseberry is missing in action this time… probably fast asleep in his duvet mound or being tenderly fed my best biscuit selection by the ever-adoring Iris.

There's nothing stopping us… just a short distance between me and him. One step would close it.

But… if we *are* going to share a Christmas kiss, do I *really* want it to happen in this chilly, grey car park? I mean… it's not exactly the setting of dreams, is it?

'Let's go adventuring!' I say, breaking the spell.

'Cool,' says Steve. 'Want to know where?'

'Go on then?' I say with a shrug, not that it'll change my mind. By this point, I'm basically happy to trot off anywhere with this man.

'Geese,' he says simply.

'What's that now?' I laugh. For some reason, my mind instantly goes to the toddler's petting zoo on the other side of town. It doesn't take me long to realise that this image is definitely not what Steve's got in mind.

'You need Christmas dinner… and my mate has geese available. And some sausages.'

'You're kidding?' I gasp.

Steve shakes his head. 'I texted him while you were dealing with the potato guy – just to check.'

'But… it's Christmas Eve!' I say. 'How…?'

'One of his biggest customers who owns a huge guesthouse folded at the beginning of the month, and he lost their order,' says Steve with a shrug. 'He's managed to sell some, but still has a whole bunch available.'

'That's… that's perfect!' I gasp. 'I mean - as long as he doesn't mind us turning up at the last minute?'

'Are you kidding me,' laughs Steve. 'It's basically made his Christmas!'

'Right!' I say, scrambling for the van. 'Let's go!'

We've only been driving for about ten minutes when Steve's phone starts to buzz in its cradle. He glances at the screen.

'It's Aunty Iris!' he says in surprise. 'Hello?'

'How are you two getting on?' Iris's voice crackles over the van's speakers.

'Great!' says Steve.

'I want to hear it from Holly,' she says.

'Great!' I echo Steve with a grin. 'We're nearly done… just getting some meat sorted out. Everything okay there?'

'All's well. I hope you've got plenty of supplies - I've just had an update from Doris. Everyone from her list is coming… and everyone I've spoken to so far has said yes too. I think Wendy's the only one who's going to be missing!'

'Well... she *is* on holiday in Australia until the New Year,' I say. 'I think we can let her off!'

'Yes... well, she's going to be very disappointed to miss it!' says Iris.

'We'll just have to make sure we take plenty of photos for her!' says Steve.

'Definitely,' I say. 'Got to keep up the tradition!' I've already got plans to start a new album – and I think I'm going to stick Iris's shopping list in with the photographs – after all, it *is* a work of art!

'Well... I hope you've got plenty,' says Iris. 'Doris has been asking people to bring along anything they fancy sharing - but we've done like you told us - everyone knows all they need to bring is themselves.'

'Perfect!' I say. 'Thanks, Iris!'

The last thing I want is for the Angels to feel like they need to brave the shops on Christmas Eve. This is meant to be a fun surprise - a treat, not a nightmare!

'We're all going to meet up at Billingham's in an hour to start getting things ready for tomorrow,' says Iris.

'You... you are?' I say.

'Of course we are!' she laughs. 'That's half the fun. You two join us when you're ready!'

'Okay... but... how will you get there?' I say.

'Doris is coming for me.'

'Alright!' says Steve. 'We'll see you in a while, then.'

'Wait - what about Arthur?' I say. 'He's welcome to

stay at mine, but I'm not sure he'd like being left alone somewhere he's not used to…'

'We'll bring him with us,' says Iris. 'I'm sure Doris won't mind if he sits in the boot of the Skoda!'

And then she's gone.

'You have no idea what you've got yourself into, do you?' Steve smirks in my direction.

'Erm… you might be right!' I laugh. 'You sure you don't mind heading to Billingham's after we're done here?'

'In for a penny!' he says. 'Anyway - in case you haven't noticed, Iris is super excited. That's the best Christmas present anyone could have given me!'

'Well… you're welcome?' I say as Steve indicates and turns down a winding, rutted lane. 'Though I'm not sure it's the done thing to make you work *quite* so hard for your own Christmas present!'

'Yeah well,' says Steve, shooting a grin at me, 'in my opinion, good things are always worth working for!'

CHAPTER TWENTY-ONE

WHEN IN DOUBT, DANCE IT OUT!
NOTHING SAYS "FESTIVELY FRUSTRATED"
LIKE A SPONTANEOUS DANCE-OFF WITH
YOUR CHRISTMAS TREE

$\mathcal{B}$y the time we get to Billingham's, the light is already starting to fade. Sure – it's only just gone two in the afternoon, but the factory windows twinkling brightly under the leaden sky.

'Are you sure you're ready for this?' chuckles Steve, pulling up right outside.

'Ready?' I laugh. 'I can't wait!'

'Good,' he says with a nod. 'Well - all I can say is - take a deep breath and get your game-face on.'

'Why?' I say, suddenly nervous.

He's staring into his wing mirror, and I wonder if he's spotted something I'm not going to want to see looming behind us... like Colin.

My stomach clenches. I've just spent a brilliant few hours with Steve - getting everything together for a Christmas treat for some of the most wonderful I've ever met. The last thing I want to do now is ruin every-thing with a show-down right outside Billingham's.

'Don't look so scared!' laughs Steve, turning to me and clearly catching wind of the fact that I'm busy tying myself up in knots.

'I'm fine!' I say, taking a deep breath.

Of course it won't be Colin!

I'm just being an idiot – and besides, I've just realised there's no reason Steve would recognise Colin even if he *was* standing right behind us. They've never set eyes on each other, and to be frank, that's the way I want to keep it!

'It's just the Angels,' he laughs. 'I think they're excited to see you!'

'How many... oh my!'

I've just caught a glimpse of the little crowd gath-ered in the doorway of the factory, waiting to greet us. When Iris said some of them were coming along to help get set up, I expected one or two at best - but it looks like we've got the full complement... as well as a couple of husbands thrown in for good measure!

'Blimey!' I laugh, clambering out of the van and turning to grin at them.

'Get the van open, there's a dear!' Iris's voice comes from the middle of the excited gaggle, and I spot her and Doris standing arm in arm, identical beams of excitement on their faces. 'We all want to get in out of the cold!'

'You haven't been waiting out here for us this whole

time, have you?' I say, horrified at the idea. 'We've been hours!'

'Course we haven't, daft girl,' laughs Doris.

'Take the boss inside for a look at what we've been up to!' says Iris, relinquishing Doris's arm and beetling over towards Steve as he opens up the back of the van.

'Goodness!' gasps Doris, peering into the packed back in wonder. 'You sure you got enough food in there?'

'I hope so!' I say, suddenly worried. 'I mean... I'm not sure we could have fitted much more in... but we could always do a second trip...'

'You know what,' says Doris, linking her arm through mine and giving it a friendly squeeze, 'I think you need to stop worrying so much.'

I grin at her. 'New year's resolution, you reckon?'

'Might not be a bad place to start?' says Doris, winking at me.

'Okay - you're on,' I say. 'Now... lead the way.'

Doris leads me away from the little crowd gathered around the back of the van - all of them intent on grabbing boxes and bags to help Steve unload.

'So... what have you lot been up to?' I say, focussing all my attention on Doris, who's practically skipping at my side.

'We managed to find all the plates, cups and cutlery, and we've given it all a good wash,' says Doris.

'Brilliant!' I laugh, 'otherwise we'd have to send

everyone home with instructions to bring their own with them tomorrow!'

I come to an abrupt standstill

'Oh… wow!' I gasp

Doris has led me straight onto the factory floor. It's been completely transformed… but I recognise the set-up from the photos in Iris's Christmas album. The long packing tables have been arranged in a huge square so that we'll all be able to eat together. They've been covered with beautiful tartan tablecloths and the places have already been set.

'Where did the linens come from?' I say.

'Gwen rummaged them out of one of the storage cupboards,' says Doris. 'They were a bit musty, so she sent her hubby home with strict instructions on how to wash and dry them. He brought them back once he'd finished ironing them!'

'That must have taken him ages!' I laugh.

'Herbie didn't mind,' says Doris with a shrug. 'He brought his gramophone and some records back with him – so that'll be fun for tomorrow!'

'Amazing!' I can just imagine this place filled with the lovely crackling tone of old records.

'Plus,' says Doris, 'it got him out of having to clear out the rest of the kitchen.'

'You've… cleared it out already?' I say.

Doris grabs my hand and starts towing me in the direction of the old kitchen. 'Look!' she says, throwing the door open wide.

'Wow!' I gasp. I've just walked into a gleaming, spotless kitchen I barely recognise. 'How... what... I mean...'

'I told them you'd be speechless!' laughs Doris.

'Where'd you magic all the stuff away to?' I gasp.

'Ah...' Doris suddenly looks a bit sheepish. 'Well... I just hope you're not going to need to get into your office between now and Boxing Day.'

I smirk and shake my head.

'Phew!' she laughs. 'I did make sure they left you a path to the desk - just in case. But the rest of it is pretty much floor-to-ceiling.'

'Well... better that it's in there out of the way!' I say. 'And... it's rather nice to have the kitchen back in action.'

'It is, isn't it,' says Doris, staring around. 'I've always thought of this as the heart of the factory. It's nice to be able to see properly after all these years!'

I nod slowly, an idea sparking at the back of my mind. Without its thick layers of dust and piles of paperwork, the kitchen seems to gleam with possibilities.

'I know that look!' says Doris, peering at me with one eyebrow raised.

'What look... I don't have a look!' I say.

'Oh - you *do!*' chuckles Doris. 'I might not have seen it on *your* face before - but it's the identical look Alf used to get whenever he'd had a brilliant idea. The last time I saw it, he'd just ordered half a ton of Reindeer Poop!'

'And look how well that worked out!' I laugh.

'A complete sell-out,' nods Doris. 'I've come to trust that slightly mad, wide-eyed Billingham stare over the years. So - as the young people say - spill!'

'Okay,' I say, staring around the space and then glancing over my shoulder just to check that we're still alone. 'What would you say if I said we should look into creating our own range again?'

'Making chocolate at the factory?' she says.

'I know - I know, it's probably a stupid idea…' I mutter.

'Not stupid. At all,' says Doris slowly. 'We'd need more staff, of course - someone to head up that side of things. But with all the new customers who've discovered Billingham's since you joined… I think it could be a wonderful thing.'

I blink at her, trying not to get too excited.

'I mean… it'll be an addition to everything we do already,' I say. 'And not at a massive scale. We'll keep it small. Manageable.'

'The hand-made touch?' says Doris.

'Precisely. Exclusive… from our family… made with love.'

'Limited edition!' she says, her eyes gleaming.

'What do you think?' I say, my stomach twisting with nerves.

'I think... I think Alf would be dancing a jig,' she says seriously.

'Thanks Doris!' I grin.

'You know what else I think?' she says.

'What?' I say.

'I think it's time to get Iris and all her happy helpers in here if there's any chance we're going to be sitting down to eat this side of New Year!'

'Erm... good point!' I laugh.

'Goodness, Holly love!' laughs Iris as she digs through our spoils from the farmer's market. 'I think you've bought enough to keep us all going for the entire month of January. And there are so many extra treats in here too!'

'Well... you all deserve it,' I shrug. 'We've had a good year - and I wanted to say thank you.'

'It's so exciting to have Christmas here again!' says Gwen, who's already scrubbing, peeling and chopping potatoes ready for the biggest mountain of roasties this county has ever witnessed.

'Absolutely!' says Iris. 'It's a wonderful idea... though we're going to have far more than we need.'

'That's okay,' I say. 'Everyone can help themselves to whatever they want to take home with them - and then we'll donate the rest to the soup kitchen in town.'

'That's a wonderful idea,' says Doris, who's busy

wrapping freshly washed and dried cutlery in the bright red napkins I bought earlier. 'They'll make good use of it.'

'I was thinking we could add some chocolates in for them to hand out too,' I say. 'What do you think? Everyone deserves a treat!'

'Well,' says Iris, 'all I can say is that I think your Gramps would be so proud of you, Holly.'

'Hear hear!' says Gwen, waving a potato at us.

'Thanks, guys!' I say, smiling at them.

'Now… enough of all this mushiness! Peel! Chop! Slice!' says Iris. 'I want to get as much prep done this evening as possible… and then tomorrow will be a doddle.'

CHAPTER TWENTY-TWO

ANGER IS JUST A TEMPORARY GLITCH IN YOUR FESTIVE LIGHT DISPLAY. FIND THE BLOWN BULB AND REPLACE IT

*S*moothing down my red jumper dress, I knock hard on Eileen's front door and step back to wait. It's a long shuffle from her armchair to the door. At least she's expecting me - I followed Iris's suggestion and gave her a quick call last night to ask if she'd join me for an outing today. After all, it *is* Christmas day... it's only fair.

After a bit of a wait, Eileen's quizzical eye peers through the gap.

'Oh Holly love, it's you!' she says.

She promptly disappears and I hear the sound of the chain being removed.

'You look wonderful!' I say the minute she reappears.

'Is it alright?' says Eileen with a broad smile. She runs a self-conscious hand over the front of her emerald green cardigan and then gives the beautiful red velvet of her skirt a little pat.

'Gorgeous!' I say.

'Well… you didn't tell me where we're going, and I don't want to let the side down!' she says. 'Now… should I wear my nice shoes or are we just going over to your place? Because if we're eating at yours, I'll change into my slippers if that's okay!'

'We're not eating at mine,' I say.

'Ooh, now I'm intrigued!' she laughs. 'So… good shoes it is then?'

I nod.

'Lucky I already put them on then, we'd be here for a month of Mondays otherwise. Those buckles are blighters to do up!' she says, shuffling onto the doorstep and clutching her smart handbag as she locks the front door carefully behind her.

'Well… Merry Christmas!' I say, as she takes my arm and lets me lead her slowly towards the car.

'It certainly is,' says Eileen happily. 'I don't know when I've been more excited. Fancy being whisked away on Christmas day!'

'Don't get too excited!' I laugh, opening the door to the car for her.

'Trust me,' says Eileen, peering up at me as I wait for her to make herself comfortable, 'compared to a tin of soup in front of the telly, spending Christmas with you is a dream come true.'

I smile at her as I close the door, and then do my

best to swallow a ridiculous lump of emotion as I head around to the other side of the car.

'Is it far?' she asks the minute I settle in next to her and get the engine running, turning all the heaters on so that we don't steam up.

'Nope,' I say.

'Ooh I'm all of a flutter,' she laughs.

'Well… it's not much,' I say, as we leave our cottages behind us and I drive us slowly through the quiet Christmas streets towards Billingham's. 'But it's just a little something to say thank you for being such a wonderful friend - guarding the house for me and making sure I'm okay with…' I pause. I don't want to say Colin's name out loud today.

'Don't you waste one more minute of your life thinking about all that, my girl!' says Eileen gently. 'If you give yourself one gift this Christmas, make it a fresh start.'

I nod. A fresh start? It's harder than I thought… but if there was ever a Christmas gift that made me giddy with excitement… this is it.

'Oh!' says Eileen, instantly distracted as we round the bend onto the road that leads to Billingham's. 'Are we going to the factory?'

I glance across at her, trying to gauge her reaction - and it's clear she's not really sure what to think.

'Well… thank heavens you didn't let me wear my slippers!' she says faintly, making me smile.

I pull up right outside, and my smile widens when I

spot Steve loitering in the doorway, clearly awaiting our arrival. There's no sign of Arthur in his Santa sweater though, so I can only imagine he's either still curled up on his duvet… or keeping an eye on proceedings. He's basically found himself in seventh heaven with all the Angels slipping him treats every five seconds.

Steve hurries to open the door for Eileen.

'Oh my,' she says with a quick look at me. 'He's even more handsome up close than he is through my binoculars!'

I splutter out a surprised laugh and Steve shoots me an amused look as he holds the door open for Eileen. I wait for her to climb out, but she looks from Steve to me and then back again.

'Have you kissed our Holly yet?!' she demands.

Steve's eyes grow wide, and I feel my face going hot as he shoots a nervous glance at me.

'Eileen!' I hiss. 'Behave!'

'At my age, why should I?' she chuckles, rummaging around in her handbag for something. 'I mean - I *am* sixty-seven, you know!'

I roll my eyes and grin across at Steve.

'Here,' says Eileen, thrusting something at him as she springs out of her seat with far more energy than I've ever seen before. Steve holds out his hand on autopilot and takes whatever she's waving at him.

I crane my neck trying to get a peep, but I can't see

a thing from here, so I hop out and hurry around to join the pair of them.

'What *was* that?' I ask Eileen, as she tucks her hand into the crook of my arm and I lead her inside Billingham's - Steve opening the door for us as we go.

'That's for me to know, and Steve to show you later… or not. His choice!' she laughs.

I glance back at Steve to see if he's going to give me any hint, but he just grins at me and shrugs. I'm about to subject my naughty neighbour to a full Christmas interrogation when her childlike squeal of delight cuts me off.

'Wow! I gasp.

'It's so beautiful!' says Eileen squeezing my arm.

When I left Billingham's earlier to change and then collect my troublesome charge, the tables were all set and ready for the revellers. However, while I've been gone a veritable woodland has sprung up on the factory floor.

'The trees?' I gasp as we both stand there, staring at the glittering forest, all with lights, baubles and tinsel twinkling. There's everything from a silver, plastic affair to a full, bushy real spruce that must be at least seven feet tall.

'We wanted to surprise you!' laughs Steve. 'Everyone brought their trees in.'

'It's gorgeous!' laughed Eileen.

I nod, though I can't quite find the words. It's not just the trees that have appeared out of nowhere. The tables have been finished off with a mishmash of paper crackers, flickering candles in holders and tea lights in jam jars. There are balloons, tinsel and paper streamers everywhere I look.

Even better than that - the room is full of laughter. There are smiling people in every direction - sitting, standing, chatting and gossiping.

'Eileen!'

Identical cheers from Gwen and Doris make me jump, and suddenly my guest is flanked by Angels.

'You know these guys?' I say with a quick look at Eileen to make sure she's not overwhelmed.

'Of course!' laughs Eileen, receiving hugs and handshakes and kisses on her cheek - looking like she's about to explode with happiness.

'But… what are you doing here?' says Doris, refusing to let go of Eileen's hand as she leads her over towards the table. I follow hot on their heels.

'Holly invited me,' says Eileen.

'We're family, right Eileen?' I say.

Eileen looks at me and I swear I see her lip quiver and her eyes grow bright for a moment.

'Right!' she says with a nod.

———

I get a resounding cheer as I appear with the first huge platter of perfectly roasted goose. Iris has already expertly carved it in the kitchen to save any chaos at the packed tables. Doris might have estimated twenty guests... but at least double that number has turned up - and I couldn't be happier.

Steve, Doris and Gwen follow with even more food, and then Iris brings up the rear with a trolley that is heaped with bowl after steaming bowl of veggies, stuffing, Yorkshire puddings, pigs in blankets and huge jugs of gravy. There's even a couple of stunning chestnut roasts for anyone who fancies them.

I can't stop my mouth from watering, and by the way everyone else is fidgeting, their eyes flicking between me and the food, their noses raised to catch the scent of the steaming feast... I've got a feeling I'm not the only one.

'Now isn't the time for speeches!' I say, plonking my plate down on the table as every eye in the place turns to me. 'Just... thank you for being here. Merry Christmas!'

'Merry Christmas!'

The cheer echoes between the trees and I shiver slightly, thinking how much Nan and Gramps would have loved this.

'Dig in, everyone!'

Bing Crosby's dulcet tones drift out through the factory doors, accompanied by the sound of laughter. Herbie's gramophone is certainly being given a good workout. Now that the meal's over, the Angels are drifting around the floor, enjoying a Christmas dance to crackling carols.

I wrap my arms around myself and take in a deep breath of chilly evening air. The day is flying by - but the party's still in full swing behind me. I've got a feeling we're nowhere near the end of our wonderful Christmas get-together just yet. Eileen's already taken a quick breather from waltzing around the room with Gwen to tell me that she doesn't ever want the day to end.

What more could I ask for?

I close my eyes for a moment, enjoying the feel of the chilly air on my flushed cheeks.

Actually… there are *two* more things I'd ask for. After all… it *is* Christmas! Number one – I wish Gramps was here to see all this. He'd have loved it. Still, we all toasted him… loudly… several times. His memory will always be kept alive at Billingham's.

The other thing… well… let's just say it's probably just as well Steve isn't out here with me right now! With all the good company, wonderful food, and at least a couple of sherries inside me… I might not be able to stop myself!

Eileen's right… the man is most definitely hand-some. Even though we weren't sitting together during the meal, somehow my eyes kept drifting towards him across the table. Every single time they did - he was looking right back at me - with a smile, a wink…

or a long look that had me fumbling for my water glass.

Blimey… I came out here to cool down a bit, but I can practically feel my cheeks glowing!

Trying to get a grip of myself, I blow a long – slightly frustrated – raspberry into the chilly air. An echo drifts up from somewhere near my feet and I glance down only to find Arthur staring back at me as though trying to apologise for his belch-snort.

'Hello boy!' I laugh, bending down to stroke his ears. 'You had a few too many treats?'

'Only enough to sink a battleship!'

I straighten up and turn, only to find Steve standing right there, holding out my scarf.

'Didn't want you to get cold!' he says, stepping closer and gently placing it around my neck.

'Thanks,' I breathe, shooting him a grateful smile.

'You okay?' he says, as Arthur leans his full weight against my leg, snuggling into me.

'I'm good,' I say. 'Just… you know… getting some air.'

He nods and stares up at the sky, following my gaze. 'No stars.'

'Nope,' I agree. 'It's meant to snow.'

'That would be fun!' he says.

I nod.

'I've got something for you,' he says quietly.

'Really?' I say in surprise.

'Don't get too excited!' he laughs. 'It's actually something we found when we were tidying up the last bits from the kitchen.'

He hands over a parcel I hadn't noticed tucked under his arm. It's wrapped in green tissue paper.

'Aunty Iris wrapped it for me,' he says. 'Hope you don't mind us nicking the paper!'

'Course not!' I laugh, taking it from him. 'Thank you!'

I tear the layers of tissue away and gaze at a chunky wooden picture frame that's divided into two with the carving of an angel.

'Doris and Iris told me you'd binned one from your office,' he says. 'We thought you could replace it with this.'

I nod, blinking hard. I will *not* cry!

'I love it!' I whisper.

Behind the left-hand pane of glass is a stunning black and white photograph - and I'm guessing it's one from Iris's collection. It shows my Nan and Grandad sitting right at the centre of a happy group of youthful Angels, husbands and children - all of them wearing paper party hats. Christmas garlands are just visible, twinkling away in the background. The right-hand pane is blank.

'We thought you might like to add your own in there,' he says quietly. 'Maybe one of the photos from this evening.'

I nod, but I can't say anything for a long moment. It's the perfect gift.

Arthur lets out a little whine, and I glance down at him.

'You okay, boy?' I say softly.

'Go on - go in,' laughs Steve.

Arthur gives a little wag and then hot-foots it back towards the factory doors. I watch him go, only to spot Iris waiting for him by the door. I give her a little wave and she returns it before blowing me a kiss and then heading back inside with Arthur.

'Sorry!' chuckles Steve. 'I think she wanted to see you getting your gift.'

'That's okay,' I laugh. 'I'm so happy right now, I don't think I'd mind if they'd all been watching!'

'Fancy coming in for a dance, then?' he says hopefully.

'In a minute,' I say. 'I want to ask you something first.'

'Oh?' says Steve.

'I was wondering... what was that thing Eileen handed you earlier?'

Steve's face cracks into a delighted grin as he rummages in his pocket. 'She said it was her emergency stash.'

'Emergency stash of what, exactly?' I ask in amusement, wondering if he's about to pull out a handful of mint humbugs.

Steve opens his hand, only to reveal a slightly crumpled sprig of plastic mistletoe.

'You're kidding me?!' I laugh.

Steve shakes his head.

'It would be a shame to disappoint her, don't you think?' he says, dangling it in the air between us.

I lock eyes with him - and this time there's nothing standing in our way - no tables full of chattering Angels or the biggest Christmas dinner I've ever seen in my life.

I take a step closer to him. We're both grinning at each other like total idiots as Steve wraps one arm around my waist, pulling me even closer.

'Get on with it!'

'Yeah - we're freezing our bottoms off here!'

We both turn in surprise, only to find Eileen and Doris giggling in the doorway, flanked by the rest of the Angels - who seem to be holding their collective breath.

I roll my eyes and turn back to Steve, whose arm is still firmly - warmly - around my waist. His eyes seem to hold a question.

'Give me that,' I laugh. Grabbing the plastic mistletoe, I hold it high above our heads and press my lips firmly against his.

It's not in the least bit romantic... how can it be when a dozen raucous cheers and wolf-whistles ring out behind us, making us pull away from each other with sheepish grins.

'Get away with you all!' Steve tuts good-naturedly at our audience.

'Spoilsport!' calls Iris from somewhere at the back

of the crowd as they all retreat into the warmth, giggling as they go.

'Hey Holly?' says Steve.

'Yeah?' I grin up at him, wrapping my arms around his neck.

'I'm going to kiss you now.'

'I thought we'd just done that?' I laugh.

'If you thought that was a kiss-'

He doesn't get to finish the sentence because I close the space between us again. My lips are on his, my hands are in his hair, and as he lifts me off my feet - I'm not sure even a bunch of cheering Angels could break us apart.

THE END

ALSO BY BETH RAIN

Little Bamton Series:

Little Bamton: The Complete Series Collection: Books 1 - 5

Individual titles:

Christmas Lights and Snowball Fights (Little Bamton Book 1)

Spring Flowers and April Showers (Little Bamton Book 2)

Summer Nights and Pillow Fights (Little Bamton Book 3)

Autumn Cuddles and Muddy Puddles (Little Bamton Book 4)

Christmas Flings and Wedding Rings (Little Bamton Book 5)

Upper Bamton Series:

Upper Bamton: The Complete Series Collection: Books 1 - 4

Upper Bamton Series:

A New Arrival in Upper Bamton (Upper Bamton Book 1)

Rainy Days in Upper Bamton (Upper Bamton Book 2)

Hidden Treasures in Upper Bamton (Upper Bamton Book 3)

Time Flies By in Upper Bamton (Upper Bamton Book 4)

Crumcarey Island Series:

Christmas on Crumcarey (Crumcarey Island Book 1)

All Change on Crumcarey (Crumcarey Island Book 2)

Making Waves on Crumcarey (Crumcarey Island Book 3)

Fool's Gold on Crumcarey (Crumcarey Island Book 4)

Seabury Series:

Welcome to Seabury (Seabury Book 1)

Trouble in Seabury (Seabury Book 2)

Christmas in Seabury (Seabury Book 3)

Sandwiches in Seabury (Seabury Book 4)

Secrets in Seabury (Seabury Book 5)

Surprises in Seabury (Seabury Book 6)

Dreams and Ice Creams in Seabury (Seabury Book 7)

Mistakes and Heartbreaks in Seabury (Seabury Book 8)

Laughter and Happy Ever After in Seabury (Seabury Book 9)

A Quiet Life in Seabury (Seabury Book 10)

In A Spin in Seabury (Seabury Book 11)

Living The Dream in Seabury (Seabury Book 12)

Seabury Series Collections:

Kate's Story: Books 1 - 3

Hattie's Story: Books 4 - 6

Standalones: Books 7 - 9

Writing as Bea Fox:

What's a Girl To Do? The Complete Series

Individual titles:

The Holiday: What's a Girl To Do? (Book 1)

The Wedding: What's a Girl To Do? (Book 2)

The Lookalike: What's a Girl To Do? (Book 3)

The Reunion: What's a Girl To Do? (Book 4)

At Christmas: What's a Girl To Do? (Book 5)

ABOUT THE AUTHOR

Beth Rain has always wanted to be a writer and has been penning adventures for characters ever since she learned to stare into the middle-distance and daydream.

She has recently moved to a windswept, Scottish island, and it is a dream come true to spend her days hanging out with Bob – her trusty laptop – scoffing crisps and chocolate while dreaming up swoony love stories for all her imaginary friends.

Beth's writing will always deliver on the happy-ever-afters, so if you need cosy... you're in safe hands!

Visit www.bethrain.com for all the bookish goodness and keep up with all Beth's news by joining her monthly newsletter!

facebook.com/BethRainBooks
twitter.com/bethrainauthor
instagram.com/bethrainauthor

.

Printed in Great Britain
by Amazon

36193462R00128